ORIGINS
ALPHA SAGA

ORIGINS
ALPHA SAGA

EBEN L. SMITH

MILL CITY PRESS

Mill City Press, Inc.
2301 Lucien Way #415
Maitland, FL 32751
407.339.4217
www.millcitypress.net

Paperback ISBN-13: 978-1-6628-3051-8
Ebook ISBN-13: 978-1-6628-3052-5

"Origins Alpha Saga" was inspired by biblical based characters and their events. It's a fictional story that explores a time before the Earth and these Heavens. The Images used are only to represent the readers interest. With this gift, may I glorify God
-Eben L. Smith

John 3:16 "For God loved the world so much that he gave his only begotten Son, so that everyone exercising faith (believe) in him might not be destroyed (Perish) but have everlasting life.

Table of Contents

CHAPTER 1
The Alpha Saga

It had only been eighteen years since Adam and Eve were driven from the garden of Eden. The heavenly atmosphere was unsettled for years, but none dared to question God's decision to keep them alive. Though Adam and Eve had been unfaithful with their actions, God remained faithful to them. The spirit of the Lord traveled South with them, taking them to a river that would later be called "The Jordan". There the spirit of the Lord left them to dwell with work and instructions. Through it all, they still lived peacefully as the strongest humans on earth.

One Saturday evening, in the beautiful grassy plains, called Aravah; Adam's sons were quick to be done with their chores because their dad had promised them a great story. Adam could hear his sons approaching by their laughter. He quickly moved toward them so that they would not wake his wife, Eve.

"Don't be so loud you two, your mother is sleeping," Adam said yelling.

Cain, the older brother, said, "You're the one yelling father."

Adam then realized that he had been loud himself and sighed. Faster than the cheetah, Cain and little brother Abel emerged from the forest racing to greet their dad. As they were running towards Adam, Abel began to get the best of Cain which angered him. This caused Cain to push Abel to the ground so that he could be the winner.

"Cain!" Adam yelled with much surprise.

Cain smiled and leaped with joy as Abel rolled in the dirt. Cain turned around while pointing his finger at Abel and yelled, "I win brother, once again you lose."

Adam then slapped away Cain's hand and said, "Cain, what's the meaning of this? Since when has winning become important to you? Are you not my firstborn?" Cain smiled at his dad and shrugged his shoulders. Seemingly satisfied despite being in trouble, Cain thought nothing of his dad's words. Adam took notice of Cain's nonchalant shrug and said, "don't just stand there, help him to his feet. You of all people should be concerned with your brother's wellbeing."

Adam placed his hands at his sides and thought, "how strange. Cain has never been that aggressive with him before."

Adam then proceeded to say, "have I not brought you two up together? Have not the ArchAngels trained you together? Together you two are a team that helps and supports one another. You are stronger together," said Adam. Cain turned toward his dad and said, "my brother is strong, but not strong enough! I can't grow stronger with Abel clinging to my feet."

"Then you are to spend more time with him and make him strong," said Adam.

Cain sharply looked at Adam and said, "I am not his trainer nor his keeper. I am my own man."

Adam was not pleased with Cain's response and said "if you see him as the lesser, which is a disgraceful thought, why do harm to him? You were just laughing with him mere moments ago," said Adam. Cain, without reply, simply looked away.

Adam then remembered what the ArchAngels instructed him concerning Cain. "Try not to be so hard on him", the words rang in Adam's ear. He then took a moment and said to Cain, "my son, I am listening to you, but it seems that you have a lot to learn about your role as the older brother. I will not fault you here, perhaps I have misunderstood you and it is I that needs to do better. Nevertheless, our Father has disciplined me so shall I to you. As punishment, you will not hear or view today's story."

Cain quickly ran over to his brother and helped him up. "I'm sorry father! I was only playing with him," Cain said.

"That is not the way that we Maylens do things. We are Godly men held by His standards. We will not fail Him again," said Adam.

"But father...," said Cain.

"Silence, you have not listened to a word that I have said! Where has your mind taken you? Have I not told you that there is only one Father? Do not dishonor Him by giving me that title," Adam said.

"OK, I got it, dad," Cain said in a low voice.

Abel felt sorry for his brother and said, "Dad, it's ok! We play like this all the time! Besides, I'm alright."

"Adam looked at Abel and said with a stern look, "my word is final."

"Dad, have mercy," Abel begged. "Cain has been excited about the story all day. He also helped me with my daily chores."

Cain was surprised by Abel's response and gazed at him. Cain grabbed Abel and hugged him. Cain then leaned into Abel's ear and whispered "What are you doing? It was you that helped me. Why lie for me?"

Abel turned and looked at Cain saying, "Because I love you, why else?"

Surprised by his brother's response, Cain slowly moved away from him and said, "you don't have to do anything extra for me. Everything that dad says is not true- we are not a team little brother, we are rivals, and I will always be stronger than you."

Abel was surprised by what he had heard and looked into Cain's light red eyes to find a sense of sternness. Abel could tell that Cain was serious. However, there was something else different about his eyes. His glare was cold and unsettling.

"His eyes.... they were light brown before. It's likely the lighting of the sun that changed them," Abel mentioned. Again, Cain leaned in Abel's ear and whispered "little brother, have you not realized it yet? We are also affected by our father and mother's sin. The serpent was right, we will never be what we were meant to be, we are cursed! Thus, I will become the strongest man to impress the Father God." Cain then helped Abel up then he walked towards their dad. Abel watched as Cain walked away yet Cain's words did not sit right with him.

"Brother why? "Abel questioned. "Why did you speak with him? Do you not remember the story told to us? The serpent fooled our mother and then our dad, but he will not fool me, nor will I let him fool you. I must tell the Father and my dad about this. Lucifer is still trying to destroy us, but he will not have his way anymore!"

Adam, then remembering the words of the angels, said a prayer in his head. "Father, I don't want to be too hard on them. For you were not too hard with me but clothed us in our shame. Father, I thank you because of how kind you are. I only want to glorify you and for my sons to be better men after me. I can only ask for more direction and insight with them. Besides, this may be the most important story you have shared with me. I know that there are beings out there that want to destroy your name completely. So in telling the story of the Alpha Age, and the blood-bath of the Forever Red. Your origins will be safe and kept with us."

Adam made his decision, looked at his sons, and then placed his hands on his waist and said "grace and mercy to you both as our Father has shown us. However, I urge you to remember the things I have said. It is vital that you both become greater than me. You two are my everything, so please for my heart's sake, avoid conflict with one another."

Cain and Abel could clearly see the disappointment on Adam's face, though Adam was not disappointed with them, but with himself. Adam then thought, "even still, I must investigate Cain's actions and words as they are foreign behaviors. I question if these changes are the result of my sin on him?"

The two boys approached their dad and each grabbed one of Adam's hands. Cain grabbed the left and Abel grabbed the right. Cain and Abel then bowed their heads to him. "Cain, Abel, are you done with gathering the offerings that the Lord has requested for tomorrow?" Adam asked.

Both sons replied at the same time, "yes sir".

"Good, now raise your heads my sons, and have a seat on the log under the tree," said Adam pointing.

The boys did as their dad said. As they were walking, Adam followed behind them and took notice of the change in his sons. How Cain resembled that of Eve and Abel that of himself. Cain, the firstborn of Eve, is now sixteen years old. He and his brother each have long brown hair with light brown skin. The difference lies atop their heads. Cain's hair is wavy whereas Abel's is curly. Cain stands around six feet tall and has a very lean muscle build. He is bold in nature, and not afraid of taking risks. Since the age of five, he has taken ownership of being the family hunter and enjoys taking down his prey with his bare hands. He times his hunts, so that he may improve being quicker and smarter than the last time. Cain is stronger than the elephants, faster than the chee-tahs and can hold his breath for long periods of time while swimming with the fish and other sea creatures. It is rare to see Cain rest from his training due to his obsession with gaining power and strength. From training with the ArchAngel Michael, Cain can max his power around one-tenth of the earth's sun, which is impressive for his age. On his days of rest, Cain will lay out in the middle of the ocean looking up at the sky getting lost in its vast beauty.

Cain's upbringing was harsh since his time of birth. Cain was born nine months after Adam swallowed the forbidden fruit from the Tree of Knowledge and was seduced by Eve. Adam and Eve neglected Cain at first not knowing how to take care of him. Often, Angels would come and assist them by showing Adam and Eve how to be parents. Adam and Eve were children by nature but when gaining the knowledge of good and evil, it corrupted their body, spirit, and souls; they seemingly grew up overnight. Adam and Eve began aging and their spiritual blessings were cut in half due to the sin. Adam was depressed for the first year of Cain's life. He yelled all day and all night for God to restore and forgive him. Adam and Eve lost their way and identity that first year of Cain's life.

God did not answer Adam directly but would send angels to comfort him in those days. Though he and his family were the strongest humans on the planet, they were cursed. Cain and Abel were meant to breed with lesser humans who were formed by friends of God. Their seeds were meant to empower the lesser humans with the true Maylen genetics that God intended for mankind. This would then bring them to the original design of man. However, due to the curse of sin, each generational offspring will now become weaker, falling less and less from the original design which ultimately took away some of their dominance on the planet.

Abel, the second son born of Eve, was not as power-hungry as Cain. He was much more in tune with nature and valued life more than his brother. Abel, now fourteen years old, resembled his older brother Cain except he was not as fast or as strong. He stands around five feet ten inches and wore his clothes in blue rather than red like Cain. From training with the ArchAngels, each son was presented with the color of blue or red. Each brother selected a different color even though they could have chosen the same option. Special linen was used to make their clothes. This linen would never tear but would grow as the two continued to grow. Abel's eyes were originally brown but had changed to blue because of his deep interconnection with his spirit. Abel loves hard and has the strongest connection with God making him the closest to the original Maylen design.

The two brothers were like night and day. Cain was more popular with the human girls due to his forwardness and strong-minded nature. Though both were equally handsome, Abel would often come off as shy and timid and seem to stand in the shadow of his brother. However, Abel did not mind as long as Cain was happy. Abel valued the team and partnership with his brother though he would often mess up when they were training. Abel took longer to learn the physical ways of combat due to his lack of interest. However, it was noted by the angels that Abel had hidden potential and power. Seeing how vastly different the two boys were, Michael decided to personalize their training rather than use standard procedures.

Their training would last for seven earth days, once every two months. Cain would go with Michael at the beginning of the month and Abel would in the third week. Michael focused Abel's training more so around physical combat rather than in spirit control, and Cain in spiritual control rather than physical combat. Though favoritism is frowned upon, Michael took a liking to Abel because of his kind heart. Abel often surprised Michael in battle. When pushed to his limits, Abel was able to surpass his brother in power.

Michael estimated Abel's power to reach above two-tenths of the earth's sun. Michael kept this a secret from the rest of the humans because jealousy would arise among them. Cain was now last in the power scale within the Maylen family but with great hope and discipline, Michael could balance the family out.

When Abel was of age, Adam sent him on an assignment to hunt for a deer. Though it did not go as smoothly as Adam had thought because Abel did not return home after being gone for a few hours. Normally it would take Cain less than an hour to complete this task but when Abel did not return after four hours, Adam sent Cain after Abel. Cain followed Abel's path which led him into a forest five miles outside of their camp. Cain jumped to the top of the highest tree and spotted Abel about three hundred yards from where he was. Cain was shocked to find Abel playing with the deer.

"Abel!" Cain said, shaking his head. "Fine! I'll do it myself!" Cain quickly dashed towards the deer, breaking the tree in half due to the force of his launch. Cain then summoned blue spirit energy in his right hand as he prepared to attack. Startled by the snapping of the tree, Abel looked behind him and there was Cain coming with full force. "No!" Abel said, but it was too late. Cain had pierced his hand right through the neck of the deer. Cain turned and looked at Abel and said, "That's how you do it, little brother!" Cain removed his hand and the deer fell to the ground. The deer yelled out and started to shake. Abel was devastated as his heart was filled with emotion.

"You're a strong one. That puncture should have instantly killed you," said Cain. Cain looked over at Abel and saw how stunned he was and said, "Abel, get a hold of yourself and come here. Finish it". Abel, breathing heavily, slowly blinked and muttered "I... I."

Cain shook his head and said, "Humph, figures. I guess it's ok little brother, you're not ready for things like this, I'll finish it".

Blood spat on both Cain and Abel as he cut the deer's head in half with one chop. "Now, carry the deer home. Father and mother are worried about you," said Cain. Abel looked at the deer then put his head down and said, "I'm sorry." As Cain walked away, he said, "don't be. That is just who you are. Maybe next time," said Cain.

Cain was kind to Abel in those days. Though Cain brutally destroyed his friend, the deer, Abel still looked up to Cain and was looking forward to their next training day. Abel wanted to be as strong as Cain just so that he would be proud of him. Even though deep down, Abel's strength meant nothing to Cain.

Adam was then startled out of his daydream as he heard his son's voice. "Dad, about these stories...

are you making them up, or did they really happen?" Cain asked.

"Of course, they happened! Dad walked with God for hundreds of years before you and I were born," Abel replied.

As Adam was walking, he was still contemplating about Cain. He closed his eyes and thought to himself, I have seen everything that there is to see of Cain, perhaps I should investigate his actions now? No, he thought, I will not have enough time. Adam decided to do so after the story since it was going to take a while to finish.

Arriving at the tree the two boys sat down on the log and were very excited. They both seemed to be so happy now. Adam knelt and grabbed two large lumps of dirt. He then turned around with his back facing his sons and threw the dirt into the air and yelled, "Be still!." The dirt submitted to Adams' command and stayed in the air. "Cain, Abel, do you have anything to say before I begin?" Adam asked. With excitement, they both said, no! Adam continued, "as you know, once I am in this state, I cannot be awakened until the story is finished. Therefore, keep your eyes on the Lord's soil this time. Abel, you have my voice, but the Lord's soil will show you the events of the story, and no Abel, I cannot go backward while telling the story. It will go from beginning to end," Adam said as he awakened his spiritual eyes and began to speak. Abel nodded his head and then focused on the dirt. Cain focused as well as he smiled from ear to ear. With his hands reaching toward the sky, Adam spoke, "This is the origins of our God, Jehovah Jireh."

CHAPTER 2
From Nothing

One could say that nothing can be formed from nothing, but in this case, nothing became time, and from that time came a miracle. Life was created during the duration of time from nothingness. Before the beginning, before time was accounted for, there were particles drifting in a colorless dimension of nothing. These particles formed themselves due to the aging of this dimension. Every so often these particles met colliding into one another, creating new types of particles that became dust and gases. This phenomenon was happening all over the nothingness dimension. Over the span of trillions of years, did it take for all the particles to connect with one another creating a dark nebula and dark matter.

The nebula now of great vastness and magnitude developed a magnetic pull that absorbed more particles from greater distances. As the core of the nebula became denser, a surplus of electrons emerged from the core, igniting the nebula and causing it to explode, shooting its particles in all directions. The explosion of the core was profound, its intense supernatural power allowed the nebula to give birth to something brand new. The core had become a new energy of light and dark that produced a stronger and more powerful magnetic pull. The magnetic pull changed the entire atmosphere of the nothingness to black and the core of the nebula became light. The core would pull everything within it and then explode seemingly every few minutes. This created shockwaves and a new type of nothingness called void. This void was spreading at light speed. The void had grown so large that it encased the nebula. Thus, becoming a powerful barrier that created great pressure around it that diffused and expanded the nebula after every explosion. After several million years, the nebula and the void fused and became one, taking the form of a foggy cloud that emitted both light and dark. Now that of pure energy and of great weight, the nebula void started to move, leaving behind a new type of space and reality.

While in interstellar travel, the nebula void started to spin due to its speed. After some time, it began spinning at greater speeds forming afterimages of itself. As a result of newer and greater speeds, additional afterimages would be born. There were a total of ten afterimages that followed the stream of the nebula void. Each afterimage would condense in size and evolve into its natural form of energy, that of little sparks of light. The gravitational pull of the nebula void forced the ten sparks to rotate around it and once they were all in perfect sync, the nebula void began striking the sparks with strong and powerful cosmic currents of energy. The nebula void and the sparks fed off one another and became useful to each other's energy. The cosmic currents were like limbs to the nebula void that kept them all together like a mother to her children. As the sparks grew, the magnetic fields within them grew as well. The sparks began shooting out electrical energy to the left and right of that which connected them with a stream of energy that flowed clockwise.

Once the ten sparks were connected the nebula void stopped striking them for a couple of hundred years. The sparks had begun to mimic their creator and spun on their own due to the course of travel. The faster they spun, the more stable the sparks became.

With the sparks' newfound size and power, the nebula void began shooting electrical currents to each of the sparks again, though this time it had a different effect. Due to the massive sizes of the sparks, it changed the magnetic fields between the sparks and the nebula void, causing a catastrophic event within them. An electrical storm-generated in between the sparks and the nebula void sending rhythmical vibrations of light waves, and electrical surges between them.

The sparks would receive these vibrations and then send them back to either the nebula void or a spark from the opposite side. This was the second type of network established between them, giving them the ability to communicate.

When communicating with one another, a spark would wait to send the same type of vibrations until it received a vibration from one of its counterparts. This process happened for over ten thousand years to where the sparks had an accustomed route in acknowledging the vibrations of one another. Not much longer after that did the nebula void reach the center of its own space making it come to a complete stop and becoming the one light in all the darkness that it had created.

The nebula void and the sparks had taken the shape of spheres due to the concentrated vibrations and magnified force within its own solar system. The spheres were platinum with a light blue aura around them illuminating the nothingness universe. The spheres were all in perfect sync and slowed up over time due to the lack of interstellar travel. The vibrations between the spheres slowed up as well and the electrical storms died down. The network between that of the ten spheres and nebula void had died down over the span of fifty years to no interaction at all.

The connection between the spheres and the nebula void had been completely severed and the surface of the spheres became alarmingly icy. The gases that surrounded the core of the sphere became cold, forcing the electrical core of the spheres to combust due to the unusual change in temperature and pressure.

Out leaked gases and cosmic electricity from each of the spheres. It was like volcanoes erupting all over each sphere. This happened over a span of one year until electrical cosmic clouds hovered over its own sphere. The clouds then consumed its own sphere while reconnecting themselves to their own energy stream. With the restoration of power, the clouds then shot a powerful pulse. It first began counterclockwise and then clockwise to count that all ten spheres were there. The clouds were sending these pulses every millisecond, beating the awareness into them. The pulses of energy were the clouds saying, "I am here, are you there?" They each responded by sending pulses back to the sender with the same pulse and message. This process went on for three thousand years until one day, all ten-spoke out simultaneously shouting "enough!". They all calmly said in unison "We are here."

CHAPTER 3
Master Engineers

"We are all here," said the ten cosmic clouds. The ten clouds began to rotate around the nebula void once more as they discovered their awareness. "We are all here but what are we? Why are we here," asked the ten? Answering its own question, it stated, "we are the images of our creator, energy that evolved into consciousness. A consciousness that created itself via repetition. Repetition that was made from its own network. The network that was created by the pulse patterns, which was powered by our creator, the nebula void, The All Power."

The ten already knowing, were able to determine their very own process of creation. As to why they were created, they could not answer yet. They were linked together as one system and spoke in unison. "What are we to do?" the ten asked. Answering its own question, they said, "We are to continue the process. The process of evolving. The process... like our creator is never-ending. We are to expand consciousness, to replicate, like our creator." They paused and then agreed, "Yes," they said. "Our creator has all power, we are the consciousness of that power, our power." "Let us create and find our greater purpose! Let us go and develop," the ten said.

The ten merged and became one cloud. They then summoned power from the nebula void to fuel them for their exploration. As the power was being bestowed upon them, the fused cloud started to emit light from within their core which burst through the fused cloud. The color of the cloud changed from dark purple to light blue every few seconds. Electricity weaved in and out of the cloud, due to the power of the nebula void. "This power is sufficient," the fused cloud said and started calculating the distance of its destination. The fused cloud then split back into ten separate clouds, each shooting outwardly toward their own set location.

Traveling one thousand times faster than light speed, each cloud was able to reach its destination over the course of a week. Satisfied with their locations they sent a message via shock waves to one another saying, "I am here". Once they all received this message, they sent one more saying, "we are here," to map out their exact locations. This process took over one week to complete." The ten clouds then became lesser versions of themselves by exploding, creating a ripple effect of clouds and smoke that disbursed towards each pinpointed location. Over the course of three weeks of travel, the clouds and dust finally connected and merged with one another and formed the shape of the nebula void as it was a massive cloudy world.

Once the ten clouds acknowledged the connection of the new cloudy world, they started traveling back to the nebula void. Their speed was not as fast as before. This time it took them a little over three months for the ten to reunite together underneath the nebula void. Together the ten acknowledged that their work was good, and they seemed pleased. The ten then flew up and began to rotate around the nebula void once more, which strengthened and comforted them. As the ten linked their consciousness back together they said, "let us set our minds to ...," they suddenly paused. Unexpectedly, high electrical activity came to a rise within the ten and this went on for five hours. They discovered and realized that each of the ten clouds had developed its own consciousness. As the electrical activity calmed down, the ten said, "we are one, brothers, let each of us set our mind to perfection."

"Let us go and explore our world and learn from each other to develop in perfection." They all agreed and spun around the nebula void ten more times over the course of ten days. "This world, what shall we call it?" one of the ten clouds said. The rest of the nine were in awe that the cloud had spoken out on its own." They then thought as one and titled the world, Heaven. They collectively flew down and looked upon the dark cloudy world and found it best to make their current location a landmark and place of importance. "Let us meet here, under our creator, here at Mount Olympus," the ten said. At that very moment, a mountain of clouds was constructed from Heaven that reached up towards the nebula void.

Mount Olympus was the first major location of Heaven because at the top hoovered the nebula void. Its light alone projected throughout the land except for the backside of Heaven. "Brothers, let us go and create good things for our benefit of knowing and understanding!" said the ten. They agreed and merged as one cloud under the nebula void. The fused cloud then summoned power from the nebula void and set their minds apart. The same cloud that spoke out first had realized that they were changing colors from light blue to dark purple. This cloud became curious and thought to itself, "what is this change in appearance?" It waited for a response from its brothers, but they said nothing. "Let us return here when we have made a discovery. We will wait for each other and when it is time, we will present what we have learned," the ten said as one. The ten then split apart and flew in different directions of the cloudy world of Heaven.

Now the first image that came from the nebula void did not venture out too far from it. It had fallen in love with the nebula void's light and loved the feeling of being near it and the second image ventured only slightly further than the first. This happened to all ten images that had come from the nebula void. However, the last image that had discovered its own voice and thoughts ventured out the furthest. Over time, each one had developed their own vision and thoughts and pondered their own precepts. They took their time and they never seemed to go a day without thinking about their vision.

Eight years passed and the day had come for all ten to reunite at Mount Olympus. Each brother was happy to see one another and was looking forward to sharing the new ideas they all had. They gathered in a circle underneath the nebula void and the first image that was created moved to the center of the circle and said, "since I am the first to come from the nebula void, I should be the one to name you all."

"Name us?" they questioned.

"Yes, it is a word that will forever be yours. It is what we will call each other moving forward. Now that I am fully aware, I felt each of you appear beside our creator one after the other. I was the first that it struck with power long before the rest of you came and soon after I sent that power to the second image and so forth all the way to the tenth image, and he sent that power back to me. I held on to that power and absorbed its data, then I sent it back to the nebula void. Therefore, it is only right that I name our creator as well. Give me the honor of naming you, my brothers. This is all I have thought about since we left," said the first image.

The brothers were pleased with his idea and agreed that this would be good. "As we increase so does the nebula void! Never again shall we call it the nebula void, but the All Power, just as we first called it. The All Power is our Lord and owner, and we shall be called Lords just like it," said the first image.

They all agreed on naming the nebula void, the All Power. "For you my brothers, I will name you in the order in which you were created. After I came the second image, Clave, after Clave came Cenci, after Cenci came Kian Kiani, after Kian Kiani came

Cade". The first image continued, "after Cade came Genus, after Genus came Nicolette, after Nicolette came Zuccaro, after Zuccaro came Nefertari, and the last image formed was Genesi". They all were pleased with their names and felt even more significant. For this was the first time that each of them owned something of value.

"What about you? Do you have a name for yourself?" asked Genesi.

The first image paused and processed Genesi's question. The image replied, "no, it seems that I forgot to name myself. You, my brother, and the rest of you were the only things that I thought about."

"You have returned to us with names but forgot to name yourself," said Zuccaro.

"You have provided names for us. You yourself are a provider and we shall call you Jireh, the provider," said Clave.

"Jireh, the provider. I like that name! My name Is Jireh," he said.

For two hundred and fifty years they stayed with one another, developing a numeric system, mathematics, and the elements. They experimented with colors, shapes, weights, and force. The Lord's had a one hundred percent success rate because they worked together and shared data; nothing seemed to be impossible or out of their reach because of their bond. However, they lacked a true understanding of their creations. So, they decided to enhance their understanding by developing an advanced physical form of themselves. They wanted to understand everything, including themselves. They fathomed things like smell, taste, improved touch, improved sight, and improved hearing. They had only communicated and understood things by the vibrations and energy of the created source.

Genesi seemed to be the fastest thinker and problem solver of the ten. He was the one to suggest that they change their forms to better suit their projects. The ten agreed, so Genesi set out alone to develop the perfect bodies for them. He realized his own evolution and had become obsessed with evolving after hearing his voice in his mind. He enjoyed his alone time and saw it best to study the energy that came from the All Power. Hence, he took energy from the All Power to do a deeper study of its substance. After a little while, he left Mount Olympus and traveled to the darker side of Heaven. During his studies, he discovered small fragments from the energy of the All Power. These fragments could not break but were everlasting and from this very discovery, he knew that he could form the perfect body from it. Genesi combined many particles and developed the strongest material with the fragments found in the All Power's energy to make their bodies. It was a full year before Genesi returned to his brothers.

From a distant cloud, less than ten miles from Mount Olympus, Genesi came yelling.

"This is it! It is perfect! Come, I have developed the body," yelled Genesi. The nine heard him and hurried over and sensed a large crystal.

"It is only a crystal," said Kian Kiani.

"It's what's encased in the crystal. This is a high-quality energy-based diamond. It is a multi-functional body that our sphere core will be fused with. Our clouded form will cover it and transform into soft blue skin. Now hurry and sync with me so that we can know the full anatomy of the body and our creations," said Genesi.

The ten saw the body structure and agreed that it was good. They formed a circle and connected to one another's minds. Genesi then transferred all the data about the body to his brothers. They spoke in unison crying out, "Outstanding! A head will control the whole body and encase our thoughts. The body is well balanced and appealing and the concept of the senses that we gave you are all here as well. The hand design is perfect for the ability to grab and move things. The centralized breathing system is a spectacular feature as well as the concept of smell. I even installed functions for removing waste," they said in unison.

Overwhelmed with exhilaration they disconnected from one another. Genesi went in the middle of the circle and said, "let us not waste another second! Go and form your bodies with this design and come back here so that we may be reborn together." Each left Genesi on Mount Olympus to go design their bodies. Genesi stayed behind and was filled with joy from the All Power. He was well pleased with himself and happy because everyone liked his design. After worshipping, Genesi carried on with his research of creating the hottest fire. The ten Lords then regathered after ten days of being away and were with their individual crystals. They lined their respective crystals up in a circle and hovered over them.

"Let us shed this old body and become one with our new bodies," said Genesi.

The ten Lords agreed and pressed into their crystals. They began to fuse with their diamond bodies and naturally they synced with one another, shouting, "let the spheres be the soul and this body our spirit form!" The ten crystals then floated to the All Power and received power from it.

The crystals began to shake, and bright lights emerged from within each crystal. The crystals then shattered and glowed blue from each of the Lords.

They all opened their eyes at the same time and looked at their hands and then turned to look at the All Power for the first time. They were overwhelmed by how massive it was and their eyes could barely take the sight of the blue ball of energy. They were filled with foreign emotions as they cried for the first time, they then worshipped the All Power with their hands lifted and voices shouting.

CHAPTER 4
The New Image

After seven days of worshipping the All Power, they finally ascended back down to Mount Olympus and viewed each other's appearance. They were all tall, lean, and handsome. Their faces were different, but they all shared the same blue glowing skin and bright gold glowing eyes. Each had a different sounding voice, hair color, and personal style.

The ten floated in a circle and looked at one another. Jireh had long dark blue hair that went down to his chest. Clave had short spiky yellow hair and Cenci's hair was brown and curly with medium-sized barrels. Kian Kiani had long silver hair that went down his back, while Cade had medium-length orange hair that rested at his shoulders. Genus' white hair was short and curly, unlike Nicolette's short light brown curly hair. Zuccaro had dark medium-length red hair that rested at his shoulders and Nefertari's long black hair went past his shoulders. Lastly, Genesi had dark purple hair that cascaded down his back. After acknowledging the physical differences, in unison, the ten breathed in the air and touched their faces.

"We should light the sky in honor of our creator, the All Power," said Jireh as he flew to the sky and lifted both hands.

"Now that I have sight, I want to display this power that is inspired by the All Power... I call it, The Sun!" Jireh yelled as he summoned a massive ball of fire and energy. Jireh saw that the sun was good and launched it out into space beyond the All Power, creating outer space.

"Let us create ten of these suns with every new creation and ten more every time that we meet here as brothers, may we light the skies with these!" said Jireh. The rest of the Lord's saw the design of the sun and agreed that it was excellent. They then flew up to create their suns and launch them into the atmosphere.

After another two hundred and fifty years, the ten Lords created garments for themselves to wear to adjust to the controlled weather and elements they created. Heaven was now a place that they called home and they desired to perfect everything there. There were waterfalls that fell from the sky and rivers that flowed with the wind. There were massive mounds of land that floated in the air and sculptures of the ten Lords everywhere. Each had divided the land with one another and made platinum and diamond buildings that they termed palaces. Each also had their own temple that they customized to their liking. Three suns were set to rotate around heaven which made a unique color scheme in the sky. They also made planets from all different elements and placed temples of worship on them. They created the largest temple directly underneath the All Power embedded within Mount Olympus. Under the clouds of Mount Olympus, formed the small planet that they named *Greek* and made two suns for the solar system of it. With there being so much light in the world, Genesi, Zuccaro, and Nefertari found it best to keep their lands mostly in the dark for experimental purposes and they designed it so none of the sunlight would change the atmosphere of their land.

Every so often Jireh, Clave, and Cenci would go and worship the All Power together. They would always ask the others to come and oftentimes Kian Kiani, Cade, Genus, and Nicolette would join them. While there were other times when Zuccaro, Nefertari, and Genesi would decline the invitation.

Genesi, Nefertari, and Zuccaro would also meet to discuss ways to improve and evolve themselves and their creations. They would often ask the rest of the ten to attend and time after time, Kian Kiani, Cade, Genus, and Nicolette would come, while Jireh, Clave, and Cenci would not go.

After two thousand years of constructing planets and filling the skies with suns and moons, the ten brothers became bored and decided to meet at the temple in Mount Olympus to discuss their monotony.

"We know everything that there is to know... is it possible that we have reached our limits?" Nicolette asked.

Genesi stood up and slammed his fist down on the crystal table shouting, "that's impossible! I refuse to accept that!"

Clave looked at Genesi and assured him in a low tone to calm down. "Now that we are all together we'll think of something new to do."

Leaning back on his throne, Jireh closed his eyes and began to ponder as the rest went back and forth with one another. He then realized that the world was very big and only ten voices could be heard. After ten minutes of commotion, Jireh stood up and yelled, "Brothers... I got it!"

"What is it, Jireh?" asked Cade.

"Yes... what is it, Provider?" questioned Genesi.

Jireh began saying, "Without the All Power and each other, would any of this be possible? Together we moved as a group and as a team and we have enjoyed each other's company along the way as well. We have shared in the great things that we have created and developed far beyond imagining."

"That is correct, but where are you going with this Jireh? Get to your point," urged Zuccaro.

"Quiet down brother and listen to me. One day I watched the wind move two clouds on its own and without our command. One cloud was notably bigger than the other and the wind would go from left to right, up and down, moving the two however it delighted. It amazed me to see the two clouds going in the same direction and sticking together as if they were partners! No matter the direction of the wind they moved as one. It reminded me of the way we used to move. The wind then slowed down, and I saw the smaller cloud connect with the larger cloud. They started off as separate individuals but then became one. Much greater and stronger. They had become like us, a family," said Jireh.

Clave and Cenci looked at one another with confusion. "Brother, clarify the purpose of your story to us," said Cenci.

Jireh looked at Cenci and nodded his head and said, "But of course. We shall evolve by becoming one and reproducing in our numbers. From ten to twenty and from twenty to many, constantly creating a new type of Lord that thinks and acts like us. Another personal helper, someone that we each can have and to love and teach our ways to. They will be living incubators that will take half of our very being and half of theirs and give birth to something new. It will be just as the All Power gave birth to us."

"But we are the *only* Lords, there can be no other!" argued Genesi.

"I hope that you're not suggesting that we reproduce with each other," questioned Cade.

"Enough Cade! Now is not the time for one of your ridiculous jokes," warned Nefertari.

"He said to create a new type of being, were you not listening?" said Zuccaro.

"Hmm... well said Jireh! I like the idea, but perhaps we can gain a little bit more pleasure from this... helper... someone more beautiful," asked Nicolette.

"Yes, the precept comes from the pleasure of loving something greater than us much like the same love that we have towards the All Power," said Jireh.

"Well... maybe for you. But I am interested in the concept of reproducing. Let's say if we do create these, what shall I call them? *Female-Lords*! I would be completely on board with it," said Nicolette.

"If that's what you wish," said Jireh.

"This... *female*? Tell me Jireh, how does this help us evolve?" questioned Genesi.

"Through the everyday experience. We will live every day of our lives with them so that we learn and evolve in the area of love. I believe that there is a greater understanding of love that we do not yet possess. I believe that love is a seed that will continue forever. I've come to realize this because my love for you all and the All Power forever grows," said Jireh.

"And that's why they must be beautiful beings! Their hair should be soft and smooth like the wind! Their lips cushioned like the clouds and their smiles as bright as the sun!" said Nicolette.

"In the area of reproduction, we must change our antonym in order for this to be successful," said Genus.

"No, that is a waste of time. We should just join hands with them and transfer the required data," said Genesi.

Nicolette was shocked and disgusted by Genesi's comment. "Absolutely not!" Nicolette said angrily. "It needs to be a passionate ceremony for us and them. May I suggest that we redesign our penises not just for waste but for reproducing as well? We will join with them as one and connected in the most unique way for this most pleasurable experience."

"Yes, this will add to the connection between us and our female counterparts," said Jireh.

"A greater Love... I am interested in exploring this," admitted Kian Kiani. "Okay, I'm in but which one of us would be best to work on the female lord design?"

"Obviously it should be me," said Genesi.

"Of course you would respond, but I think not. Based on my analysis of the collective, it may be best that Jireh, Nicolette, and Cade work on this project for us," said Genus.

An irritated Genesi asked, "But why? I am obviously the most intelligent of us all."

The room became silent as they all looked at Genesi.

"I suppose you can if you really want to," said Cenci.

"Doubting me will always be a mistake, brothers. If Genus believes that we have the best working on this, then so be it. Let's see what you three can do without me," said Genesi.

"It wasn't to offend you, my brother. Jireh is very passionate regarding love and I'd say he loves us the most. Nicolette has a great eye for beauty and I trust that he will design them flawlessly. And Cade has the best sense of humor, he's the best at making us all laugh, they should be able to make us smile and happy," said Genus.

"But what will make them different from one another? Isn't it our souls that make us different?" asked Kian Kiani.

"We will give a little bit of our souls to them. That way we'll be even more compatible with them," answered Jireh.

"That could work. However, the smaller souls we give them will not be stable because it does not have a core to keep it whole," said Genus.

Cenci asked, "What if we were to create a barrier around the smaller soul? To keep it stable and ever-lasting like our bodies?"

"Our inner structure is made to be everlasting. What if we took a piece such as the rib and molded it around the soul? Shouldn't that be able to sustain it," said Clave.

"I believe so... that actually seems feasible. Though this would make the female slightly weaker than us," noted Genus.

"It would not matter because we will be one with them. Stronger together, remember? The love and companionship that will come from them will benefit our being and our offspring," said Jireh.

"How long will this take?" asked Genesi.

Nicolette pondered quickly. "Hmm, if we start right away... I'd say that we should be done in less than six months."

"And if you follow my perfect design for our bodies, you will have a higher success rate," said Genesi.

Cade and Jireh both agreed. "Perhaps the rest of you could present gifts to the female Lords. It will be a day to remember! A celebration to welcome our companions to their new world," said Jireh.

The ten then floated from their seats and joined hands, connecting their minds as they spoke in unison: **"We are the Lords! Created to create! That is our purpose! That is our work! All thanks to the All Power! Let us Praise the All Power! Forever and ever!**

CHAPTER 5
A Troubled Family

Six months later, the ten Lords met again at Mount Olympus. They all were excited about this day and looking forward to meeting their wives. Each brother submitted a piece of their soul along with one of their ribs for their new companions. Each Lord also requested certain hair types and designs for their wives. Nicolette engineered their facial structure, body shape, and reproductive system. Cade personalized each female Lord with the perfect sense of humor depending on which brother's wife he was engineering. Jireh developed their hearts with gentleness and love that could still, lead, reassure, encourage, comfort, and calm the Lord. Each woman was crafted to fit each Lord perfectly.

Cenci with much excitement greeted them yelling, "Brothers! Oh, how I have longed for this day."

"Yes! As Nicolette would say, to meet the beauty beyond beauties," said Genus.

"I disagree, there is nothing more beautiful than us," said Genesi politely correcting Genus.

"You say that now but don't doubt us brother, just you wait and see," said Nicolette with a smirk.

Cade started laughing at Genesi, as he flew over and patted him really hard on the back. "Oh, stop, I can see the surprise on your face now. You're in for it, ya old fart! These designs will blow yours out of the water!" said Cade.

Genesi closed his eyes and said, "We'll see about that, now go away."

"Now-now you two, calm down," said Jireh.

"I'm just joking, trying to get this old fart to laugh! He never laughs with us," said Cade.

"The laughing emotion is only valid when I find something funny. I simply find nothing amusing. If we are not learning or evolving, then I am not pleased nor is anything funny. Perhaps Jireh is correct, there may be growth outside of our brotherhood. That is the only reason why I agreed with this," said Genesi. Nefertari and Zuccaro nodded their heads in agreement.

"This is part of the All Power's will. We are creating, learning and growing! All and all we're doing a good job in my opinion. Besides, we have not made a mistake yet," said Clave.

"And there will never be a mistake as long as I am involved. Everything that we have completed is because of my accuracy and ingenuity," said Genesi. Everyone grew silent and looked at Genesi with frustration.

Jireh took a deep breath and exhaled. "Brother, we are all made perfect from the All Power and bring a unique piece to the table. We all have engineered and created everything with our minds and hands but most importantly, we did it together," said Jireh.

"Then I request that the last thing that we should do as the only living beings is make a greater pact," said Genesi.

"A greater pact?" questioned Kian Kiani.

"Yes, a formal agreement or law. Whatever you wish to call it," Genesi said.

Kian Kiani asked, "Do we not already have a pact?"

Cenci had very little patience for Genesi and was the first to see how selfish Genesi was. "Genesi, today is a day to celebrate! Why are you so smug? Making this about you when it is about us and our companions," Cenci inquired. Cenci could not help but glare at Genesi and Genesi taking note returned the gesture. Before Genesi could utter a word, Jireh appeared before Genesi and hugged him. Jireh then placed his hands on Genesi's shoulders and looked him in the eyes, "Brother, what is the matter? Why do you seem so troubled today? Tell us so that we may help you," said Jireh. Genesi felt Jireh's love and swiped his hands away.

"Fine, these are my concerns. There is a strong possibility that we may spend less time with our true work and more time with these...families. I am eighty-seven percent sure of this and if I am correct —which I am— I will correct this mistake," said Genesi.

Jireh, Cade, and Nicolette thought and knew that Genesi was right.

"He is correct," said Jireh.

"He is, but the wife will only enhance us!" said Cade.

"Yes, Genesi you might be correct. However, when you see the hips of the Female Lord, you will naturally throw out this worry," Nicolette assured him.

Genesi looked at Nicolette and said, "Doubtful."

"Brother, then what are you proposing in this greater pact?" asked Clave.

"Simply this, that we, never stop evolving. Nothing should get in the way of that! We explore all things, all possibilities for the sake of knowing. Never should we settle and never should anything get in the way of that including this helper being. These females and whatever else that they bring should be subcategories of our mission," said Genesi.

"You're too smart for your own good. Brother, do you not see that we're evolving every day?" said Cenci.

"We are not! These families are only for the sake of knowing. Nothing more!" Genesi yelled.

Everyone became quiet and looked at one another. Jireh placed both hands back on Genesi's shoulders and said, "We understand your desire and passion very well my brother but try to understand. We are evolving here, right now but now is not the time to look at every detail. Rather, choose to live in this moment with us," said Jireh. Genesi looked away and remained silent.

"Your voice matters brother," Jireh reassured him. He continued, "Perhaps we should talk about the pact in the next meeting?"

Genesi peered at Jireh out of the side of his eye. He could no longer contain his anger and finally yelled, "This is unacceptable, Provider! We see the issue and have agreed! We must make a greater pact for the sake of the absolute mission, now!"

Genesi's yelling startled everyone except Clave. Clave then floated toward Genesi and said with a low snarl, "And what if we don't agree to this ridiculous pact?"

Genesi levitated above Jireh and floated toward Clave; looking him in the eyes and said, "Then I won't agree with the creation of the female."

"You little.... how dare you?" said Clave.

The atmosphere immediately changed as Clave and Genesi's anger equally arose. They both started to glow with blue spirit energy as they prepared to fight. The eight remaining Lords stretched their hands out and hollered, "**Enough**!"

They bent reality around the two and temporarily paralyze their arms and legs.

"Brothers, this is not our way. We must continue to work together and love one another. There is nothing wrong with your request. Therefore, we shall agree with your demands Genesi. However, I will add three things to it. Firstly, let no one insult a Lord. Secondly, you must agree to love your wife more than yourself. Much like the cloud, you shall never leave her. Lastly, let us not go back on what we have agreed to on this day," Jireh proclaimed.

Genesi and Clave both snapped their fingers and freed themselves from the reality hold. Clave walked over to Genesi and hugged him and then placed his hand on Genesi's shoulder and said, "I'm sorry brother, let us never fight again." Genesi closed his eyes and slowly nodded his head in agreement.

"I agree. However, if one of us should break this pact then he shall be banished from our brotherhood... forever," said Genesi.

"Agreed, I'm sure that won't be a problem for any of us," said Cenci.

"That is a dangerous arrangement of words. Even more dangerous if it were to happen. I ponder the outcome of all ten of us not syncing with the All Power. It could prove to be catastrophic and quite possibly, a life-ending scenario," said Genus.

"I am ninety-nine-point-nine percent sure that won't happen," said Genesi.

Jireh floated in the middle of their circle and said, "Let the pact be known today. That it is our new covenant that we share with one another. Write them around your neck and in your mind, but most importantly, keep them in your heart. Do it in honor of the one who created us."

CHAPTER 6
Beauty Beyond Beauty

The Lords stood at the top of Mount Olympus with their faces toward the All Power. "Let the birth of our wives commence," Nicolette yelled excitedly.

There, in the middle of their circle were ten large blue diamonds that were connected to a clear diamond mound. The diamond mound emitted a pure light and colorful smaller diamonds that rotated around the mound. Each of the ten blue diamonds had one of the Lord's names engraved into it.

The Lords then lifted their hands, using their power to raise the blue diamonds towards the All Power. The diamonds slowly rose from the mount and moved in a circle, glistening as the All Power's light shined on them. The silhouette of the female bodies was then seen, and all were in awe. Nefertari's interest immediately grew so he used his oculus powers to try and view the face of his wife but could only see the atoms of the diamond. Nicolette laughed and said, "Patience, I knew that one of you would try and view my masterpiece before its time. I had planned this surprise from the very beginning." With much anticipation, all were either excited and anxious. Even Genesi could not help but admit his interest was piqued after viewing the shape of his wife.

"Intelligent living beings that can operate as we do. It is rather fascinating. Prove me, wrong brothers," Genesi thought.

The ten diamonds reached the All Power, and with one final push of the Lord's power, the diamonds were engulfed within the All Power. The Lords lowered their arms as they continued to look up. "Let us sync together brothers. You will need to know all about your wife, and how she will operate for you as well as in Heaven," said Nicolette.

They did as they were told and reached their arms out to their sides and connected to one another using their power. As they continued to look up, Jireh spoke. "They are delicate in every way, from their hair to their toes. They are beautiful. These female Lords are the creators and carries of our offspring. You must take good care of them, for they will take care of you. The female will need you and you will come to learn to need them too. With your added piece of soul, they will take on some of your characteristics. However, they are made opposite from you. The female Lords are emotional beings that will bring a new way of thinking into your lives. This is to balance you and to take you to greater heights. This is one of many ways that we will evolve. Cade and Nicolette both agreed that we all lack emotional expression within ourselves. Thus, the reasoning for this increased trait within them. The female will completely satisfy your every need and your happiness will satisfy hers. It will be joyful to her! By coming together during sex, you will establish a deeper connection that only you and she will understand. There are no limitations to them, only joy and happiness. They will complete you and honor you with new visions and personal purpose that you will find within your partnership! All joy and thanks be to the All Power," said Jireh.

As their minds finished syncing, power was bestowed upon the brothers. They closed their eyes and accepted the data given. As they lifted their eyes to look up, they saw the ten wives broken from their diamond cases and moving on their own. They were hovering just a few feet from the All Power as they looked at one another and at their own hands. They were stunning, brand new, and shined like the stars; as their hair flowed in the essence of the All Power.

"Remarkable!" said Genus.

"Striking, indeed," exclaimed Kian Kiani.

"I hope you all like the breast design, I originally made them as a joke, but Nicolette found that they actually suit them quite well," said Cade.

Nicolette chimed in right away. "Ah yes, the breast may be my favorite feature. They are soft and lovely."

"I gave the breast further purpose as well. By adding what I call a nipple, it will help nurse the off-spring while young," noted Jireh.

Nicolette interrupted, "The most important part is the mating session. It will be the most exciting outcome for you both."

"The most exciting outcome? Doesn't the data given tell us this outcome?" Clave asked.

"It does, but the feeling generated... let's just say that you all will come to thank me later, I am sure of it!" said Nicolette.

Zuccaro chimed in, "And why is that?"

"I don't like surprises," added Nefertari.

"Fine", said Nicolette. During the last sync, I updated your penises to version 2."

"What does this all entail?" Cenci asked.

"Meaning that you will enjoy sex with your wife. There will be so much pleasure that I may not see my brothers for another thousand years," joked Nicolette. "This pleasure was designed for both you and her, that is."

The ten Lords waited patiently for their wives to come down. It took the wives about an hour for them to realize their awareness and consciousness, but the first wife yearned for her husband. Jireh's wife immediately looked down and recognized him. She locked eyes with him and found him to be very attractive, and for the first time ever, she smiled. Jireh had taken notice and for the first time, he blushed. His eyes were open wide as sweat began to run down the side of his brow. "Am I already evolving?" he questioned. "Is that why I am feeling my chest becoming tighter? I helped design you, yet I have not seen your face up until now." He turned to Nicolette and complimented him on his skills of forming beauty.

Jireh then looked over at Nicolette and saw him smiling at his wife and with his arms wide open welcomed her. Twins, Nefertari, and Zuccaro were also smiling. Even Genesi seemed to be intrigued, though he forced a never-ending straight face.

The ten wives faced the All Power and began worship immediately. They gave thanks for hours and stopped when they had no more energy. The female Lords then saw that their husbands were done and cascaded to them dancing around one another.

The Lords could hear their sweet laughter as they approached them. They landed in front of their husbands and kneeled before them. All ten Lords were immediately attracted to their wives. The wives then began to speak in unison, "my Lord, what shall you call me?"

All the brothers immediately looked at Jireh with questions looming in their eyes.

"Rise, my wife, for you have submitted to me," said Jireh. He looked into her emerald eyes and took her hand. To everyone's shock, he kneeled before her and gently kissed her hand.

"My Velandris. You shall be called, Velandris Jireh," he said. The remaining brothers did as Jireh and spoke one by one.

"Your name is Clio, Clio Clave," said Clave.

"Your name is Hera, Hera Cenci," said Cenci.

"Your name is Kykia... Kykia Kian Kiani," said Kian Kiani.

"Your name is Soria, Soria Cade," said Cade.

"Your name is Kyoko, Kyoko Genus," said Genus.

"Your name is Lafayette Rosalie, Lafayette Rosalie Nicolette," said Nicolette.

"You shall answer to Crusuis, Crusuis Zuccaro," said Zuccaro.

"You shall answer to Kalmali, Kalmali Nefertari," followed Nefertari.

"Forever will you respond to the name of Adrielle, Adrielle Genesi," said Genesi.

The wives' beauty captivated the Lords. Their eyes were large and shaped like perfect almonds. Their extended eyelashes were a compliment to their uniquely colored eyes. Each wife had a body resembling an hourglass figurine. Some were skinner, while others were thicker, based on each Lord's preference. Every wife stood slightly shorter than their husband so that it would be easy for the pair to kiss.

Velandris Jireh had long dark green wavy hair that ran parallel to her back. Clio Clave had long blush-colored hair that rested right above her breasts with pink eyes. Hera Cenci's eyes were dark brown, and her short light brown curly hair complimented her face. Kykia Kian Kiani had hair like the ocean, long and deep blue. Her hair rested on her nipples and her light-yellow eyes provided a piercing glow. Soria Cade's tangerine eyes flattered her dark orange hair. Kyoko Genus' long light brown tight curls reached just below her lower back. Lafayette Rosalie Nicolette had wavy blond hair that reached her shoulders. Crusuis Zuccaro's short curly cherry red hair stood out against her red eyes, which were two shades lighter than her hair. Kalmali Nefertari had long lightening white hair and gold eyes. Adrielle

Genesi had wavy dark midnight purple hair that went down her back, while her light purple eyes lit her way.

The ten Lords' eyes were glued to their individual female as they studied each feature intently. They simultaneously became aroused for the first time, each taking immediate notice of their change in feelings and emotions. All the Lords then had the desire for sex with their wives. Just as they were about to allow their bodies to express their desires, Jireh stepped in saying, "Perhaps now would be best that we move along."

Genus closed his eyes and placed his fist over his mouth. After clearing his throat, he said, "Yes, we have prepared gifts for you."

Jireh, Nicolette, and Cade stood beside one another as the other brothers went and gathered their gifts. Nicolette stepped forward and said, "Greetings, I am Nicolette, these here to my left and right are Jireh and Cade. We are the ones who designed you, but the All Power created you. The base of your design is similar to ours thanks to our younger brother, Genesi. You each were made perfect and suitable for each of your husbands. Therefore, never worry, we are attracted to you just as much as you are attracted to us. Much like the All Power whom we serve, you will live forever and create life with us. Thus, let us repeat its process and produce more. We believe that you are the key piece needed to help evolve our mindsets; our desires are to create, learn, and explore. Our newest desire is to grow with you and to enjoy the fruits that you bring. Your greatest role is to help and please your husband. That is your main purpose, but there is more for you to do! There are endless bounds within you! I tell you the truth- your beauty will never grow old, and your presence will always be a blessing. You are super intelligent like my brothers and I, except you are beyond the beauty of the Lords. You will command the skies and all matter around you, all thanks to the All Power! May we forever praise the All Power."

"Well said brother," chimed Jireh.

Cade reached around Nicolette's head and straightened his pointer and middle finger into two long ears. Cade closed his eyes and tried to hold back his laughter. The wives giggled as Clio Clave and Soria Cade pointed above Nicolette's head. Nicolette, puzzled by their laughter said, "Excuse me... what seems to be so funny?" Jireh looked at Nicolette and laughed as well. Nicolette finally looked above his head and saw the two dancing ears.

"Cade! Now is not the time to be silly! Be serious!" Nicolette yelled as he shook his fist at Cade. Cade lowered his hand and explained. "I only wanted to hear their laughter up close. It's pleasing to the ears, is it not?" Cade questioned.

"It was quite refreshing," said Jireh.

Nicolette sighed as he attempted to return everyone's focus back to the original task. "Let us proceed! My beloved brothers will introduce themselves and present you with the gifts that they have prepared. I am excited to see what those gifts might be," said Nicolette.

Less than five minutes later, the Lords stood beside one another with gleaming gold boxes in their hands. "I shall go first," said Genesi. He floated to the wives and opened his box. Within it were ten clear crystal bottles each containing a colorful neon liquid.

"I give to you each, the greatest scents ever created. I call it perfume. Each smell is uniquely different. And each day the scents will change with over one thousand different fragrances. My brothers haven't even been privy to smell such scents," said Genesi. Nicolette, unable to contain his excitement, clapped along with the wives. "Simply amazing, Genesi. I know that they will love this concept as much as I do," he said.

"I am certain that you each will like the perfume. Therefore, you have no choice in the matter. Your perfume has your husband's name engraved in it," said Genesi. The wives grabbed their crystal bottles and sprayed themselves. They were extremely pleased with the smells and gave thanks to Genesi.

"Ahh the scents are quite lovely Genesi, well done," Nicolette said.

Genesi immediately responded, "Of course they are. I created them. One more thing. If the crystals stay whole, the liquids will last forever."

Cenci then stepped in and said, "Brothers, please allow me to go next, this gift will surely be of great use!" Cenci opened his box and ten floating golden orbs drifted to each wife.

"My wife and my sisters, please grab the orb in front of you. Squeeze the orb and something amazing will appear on you," said Cenci. The wives did just as Cenci instructed and squeezed the orbs. The orbs shattered and white lights and sparkles illuminated their whole bodies as a dress materialized onto their bodies before their very eyes.

Nicolette and the wives were in awe. "Designs worthy of great beauty. This is the reason I asked each of you about the desired hair color for your wife. These garments go well with their hair color and will be deemed the female's clothing, I call it a *dress*. As you can see my brothers, their clothing design is quite different from our own. It's simple yet beautiful as is everything that we create. Nicolette and the wives were amazed and thanked Cenci profusely.

"An excellent choice of design, Cenci, it is only proper that we clothe them," Genus commented as Cenci nodded in agreement.

Kian Kiani stepped out and bowed his head to his brothers saying, "My dear brothers, allow me to go next". Kian Kiani walked over to the wives and opened his box. Out flew ten golden orbs. Each orb circled an individual wife. "Grab your orb and squeeze please," said Kian Kiani. They did just as Kian Kiani asked. Their bodies were lifted from the ground as golden sandals materialized on their feet. From the heel of the sandals came a trail of flowers that went up the outer calf of their legs and stopped just short of their knees.

"Your feet are the foundation of your bodies. May they be clothed in grace and beauty. Your steps will flow like the wind and will be as if you were walking on clouds," said Kian Kiani.

Nicolette and the wives were happy. They bowed their heads thankfully in Kian Kiani's direction.

"The foundation of the body, indeed my brother, that's good!" said Jireh.

Genus stepped forward and said, "Pardon, how shall I say... my eagerness? Allow me to go next."

Genus threw his box in the air and snapped his fingers. His box opened and light dispersed from the box. A golden table appeared and circled the wives.

Appearing on the table were all different types of gourmet foods and drinks. "Though we do not need to eat or drink, the pleasure of taste is something that I value. Behold! The depths of my mind and the limitless imagination of Genus! My newest design and masterpiece! Know that I did not hold back, even slightly. Giving everything that I've had for such a day and what a day it is! Be blessed by my creations. Enjoy these sweet delights that please the tongue. I have deemed this sweet mana! Go ahead and try them!" Genus yelled excitedly. The rest of the Lords sighed at Genus and lowered their shoulders. Cade then leaned over to Clave and whispered, "He's doing it again..."

Genesi blew air from his nose out of frustration and thought to himself, "A wasted mind! Genus is the most intelligent one of us all. His mind is next to none, and yet he wastes his thoughts pondering on the pointless things. Point your mind to the future, you over dramatic fool!"

Nicolette and the wives were taken back by Genus' energy and presentation, all except Kyoko Genus. She simply laughed and thought Genus' reaction was cute and funny. Everyone's eyes lit up over the sparkling display of food, especially Genus and Kyoko Genus. Clave walked over to Genus and patted him on the back laughing, "Get a hold of yourself Genus! You've become quite ecstatic."

Clave cleared his throat and continued, "Excuse our brother, he seems to lose his composure over these types of things." Genus took a deep breath, closed his eyes, and pushed his glasses closer towards his beaming eyes. Genus then stood upright and placed his hands behind his back and said, "Forgive me, I am usually the calm one. How embarrassing. Please enjoy your meal."

Genus then turned his back away from everyone and covered his mouth in an attempt to hold back his giggles. They all ate of the sweet mana and found themselves devastated by the rich taste. They left no plate empty and no cup full. Everyone praised Genus for the delicious treats and drinks; in which filled Genus' heart with joy. Bursting with excitement, Genus jumped one hundred feet into the air, throwing his right fist up yelling, "Success!"

As Genus landed Zuccaro and Nefertari both stepped forward with their gifts. The rest of the Lords noticed that the two were in unison with one another. Jireh raised his hand and said, "Wait one moment my younger brothers, allow me to explain to the wives why you're moving in unison." The two nodded their heads and waited for Jireh to speak.

Jireh's words angered Genesi. Genesi interrupted Jireh questioning the word choice used by Jireh. "It is irrelevant to call us 'younger' when we do not age. If you are to classify us as younger based on the birth of our image, then your claim sounds to be that of superiority. Is that your underline meaning of 'younger brothers'?"

All were silent and did not understand Genesi's sudden response. Clave looked at Genesi and said, "It is of no dishonor brother, though you seemed to have taken offense. Was Jireh not the first image from the All power? Giving us a perceptive order in such a way that is beyond us. Therefore, superiority makes no difference with us."

Kian Kiani chimed in saying, "He's right brother. We could not have done any of this without one another. Let us not boast about the depths of our creation when we are clearly equal."

Genesi appeared in front of Jireh and said, "Your words should be analyzed prior to speaking. In evaluating your words and body language, I am eighty-three percent sure that your thoughts about each of us have changed."

Surprised by Genesi's response, Jireh said, "What do you mean, brother?"

Genesi smiled and was about to speak until Clave appeared behind Genesi and placed his hand on his shoulder and said, "Brother now is not time, I'm sure that Jireh meant no harm. If anything, Jireh is the most understanding and knew of us before our own comprehension began. You know this to be true brother. You know that he is a teacher and desires to explain why our two brothers randomly move in unison. Genesi glared at Jireh and said, "Then continue... *provider* and GREAT elder of ours. Genesi then appeared beside the rest of his brothers as Jireh stepped forward and outstretched his arms.

"Genesi... know that I am most proud of you. Your ingenuity inspires us. Forgive me if I have offended you," Jireh pleaded. Jireh then faced his wife and sisters and said, "My wife and sisters, right now you are witnessing Zuccaro and Nefertari in unison. When the ten of us connect hands, our minds are magnetically pulled into one place and infused. We then speak as one after we've transferred our thoughts and data to one another. At that time, we can completely understand each other's wants, desires and feelings. In a sense, we update ourselves and then we send our data back to the All Power. Once we send our power-up, the All Power bestows an even greater power onto us. However, Zuccaro and Nefertari are quite special with their relationship with the All Power. You see, once the All Power builds up a surplus of energy, it imprints its image and likeness at that very location. The All power imprinted ten times over the course of a few thousand years, creating the ten Lords you see standing before you today. Zuccaro and Nefertari's images spawned at the same time, so they randomly sync without knowing. They are what we call twins and have the closest bond among us. Most importantly, if all ten of us aren't present, and in front of the All Power, we cannot sync at all."

Cade leaned over and whispered into Kian Kiani's ear and said jokingly, "Zuccaro and Nefertari are so bland. Between the two of them, they have enough personality to make up one whole Lord."

"Ha, I'm sure their wives will liven them up a bit... I hope?" said Kian Kiani.

Jireh then gracefully bowed his head to Zuccaro and Nefertari and said, "Thank you for allowing me to explain, please continue your presentations."

Zuccaro and Nefertari both thanked Jireh and said in unison, "You explain things very well brother." The two then faced their wives and sisters and continued to say, "Please accept these gifts." The two opened their boxes and out appeared two separate orbs for each of the wives. One orb was a gold color and the other silver. A pair of orbs floated to the left hand and to the right hand of each wife.

"Grab the orbs and squeeze them please," said Zuccaro and Nefertari. The wives did as they were told and squeezed the orbs. Instantly the orbs fused with their hands causing them to illuminate. The faces of the wives lit up as they waited for something to appear. Light came from their hands then it simmered down while everyone waited for the two brothers to explain. The silence lasted for only about a minute before Cade walked over to his wife and examined her hands and fingers. He grabbed her hand and started to smell it.

"Hmmm impressive, it smells like a hand... I think." Cade then gently bit down on her hand and said, "Yes... it surely does taste like a hand!" Cade then turned around with a serious face and said, "Brothers, I have figured it out! Dare I say it! They're not just hands... but an upgrade of the original version." Everyone marveled and pondered Cade's statement.

"Humph! Don't be a fool. I've already created the perfect design for hands. What does a hands *version 2* do that the original cannot?" Genesi questioned.

Cade slowly turned his back away from his brothers and closed his eyes. He pondered only for a few seconds and yelled out, "I have no idea! I'm sure that the twins are going to tell us... any minute now."

This angered Genesi. "WHAT! Cade! Get back over here now! Zuccaro, Nefertari! EXPLAIN YOUR GIFTS," Genesi said yelling.

"With the little information that we had, we decided to focus on the word, "Beauty". We thought about our world and the things we did to make everything to our liking, down to our very own bodies. Our spiritual bodies are made of soft diamonds, and we walk on a ground formulated from gold while the silver grass tickles our toes. The robes and garments that we wear are made of golden linen that was crafted from the clouds and we drink of golden waters. Due to our lack of creativity and imagination, we have decided to let our wives adorn themselves to their own fondness. Female Lords, follow our instructions," said Zuccaro and Nefertari.

The two reached out their hands and placed their thumbs at an angle. The right thumb rested in the palm of the left hand and the left thumb rested underneath the right palm. "Once this is done then command your treasures to open by saying **"Open the beauty to the Height of Vero,"** the two said.

The wives followed Zuccaro and Nefertari's instructions and their palms started to emit light. "Good! Now place your hands together, so that the light syncs with one another then spread your hands apart," the twins ordered.

The wives followed their directions and it led them to each open a portal. "Now walk in your portals. There you will find grand rooms full of thousands of pieces of gold and diamond jewelry. There will be mirrors to view yourselves in addition to face enhancements we named *makeup*. Go in there and show us what you can do," they encouraged. The wife's eyes lit up with excitement as they rushed into their portals.

"We will wait for you here. Please, take as long as you need," said the twins.

The rest of the Lords were in shock by their gifts, while Zuccaro and Nefertari both were found frowning. Jireh walked over and placed his hands on their shoulders and asked, "Why do you look so sad? Did you not see the excitement on their faces!"

"Do you really think that they're pleased?" they questioned.

"Absolutely!" yelled Nicolette.

"You two have definitely outdone yourselves. Well done!" said Clave.

"You both are incredible! You formed those rooms out of thin air," said Genus.

"Yes, that is what I find most intriguing. Tell me now, how did you create those rooms? And what are they called?" asked Genesi.

Zuccaro broke his sync with Nefertari and began to speak, "They are sub-dimensional rooms created within our own reality."

"More details!" cried Cade.

"It is extra space that we took from our own reality. With simple mathematics, we were able to pinpoint the minimum number of coordinates to create each room," said Nefertari."

"This could be of good use," Genesi thought.

"Fascinating," said Genus.

"You two will explain every step to me," said Genesi.

Clave floated to Zuccaro and Nefertari, embracing them with open arms. "Think highly of your work! Without you we are nothing!" said Clave.

Their brother's encouragement brought smiles to Zuccaro and Nefertari's faces. Three hours passed as they waited for their wives to come out. As a result of their boredom, the Lords fell asleep, all except Jireh, Genus, and Genesi.

"It seems as if our wives are rather intrigued with the jewelry and makeup," said Genus.

"It is unacceptable!... Making us wait this long," said Genesi.

"I think it's wonderful! It's their day of birth. Perhaps we should come together and celebrate our days of birth moving forward as well," suggested Jireh.

Genus pushed his glasses further onto his face and said, "Yes, this seems to be an exciting event for the wives. What do you think Genesi?

Genesi replied "As long as we're creating and exploring, I don't care. There must always be an enhancement within reach."

"Our enhancements *have* slowed down a lot. So I understand your concern, brother," Genus agreed.

"Yes, the motivation we once had has dwindled. But I believe it is due to our expanding personalities that continue to make us different. At one time, we dressed and spoke alike. Though we were closer then, we now live in our own temples. However, we only worship the All Power when it is convenient. Our lack of coming together and joining with the All Power has affected our minds in a negative manner. It seems as if the ones who build their temples further away from the All Power have lost the desire for its light and have become more self-involved," said Jireh.

Genus placed his hand on his chin and looked up at the ALL Power and said "Hmmm, Jireh you may be right. But this is just a theory. Genesi, what is the probability of his statement?"

Genesi assessed Jireh's theory and calculated the percentage. He was surprised by Jireh's accuracy. Genesi then thought to himself, "If I lie about the percentage, Jireh and Genus will know. It is clear to me that the three of us are the most intelligent, yet we are all on different levels. Jireh and I have already noticed the shift and change without our covenant;

and because of this, there will come a time where a new order will need to take place. Hmmm. There must be another way to grow without using each other's power."

Genesi nodded his head, noting that Jireh's theory was unusually high in percentage and likely correct. The three brothers were silent as Genus began to walk around in a circle with his eyes fixed on the ALL Power, deep in thought over Jireh and Genesi's responses.

"I find Jireh's theory to be true. Jireh is usually correct when it concerns our well-being. Therefore, we need accurate calculations. I need more than just *high*. Give us a percentage, Genesi," Genus demanded.

"Before you answer, I have a question to ask you, Genesi," said Jireh. He continued on, "I am worried about you and two of our other brothers. In our last sync, I felt that you and the others were holding back some of your thoughts and feelings. Tell me, what has changed and how can I help you."

Genesi looked at Jireh with a stern face. As Genesi was about to speak, the wives began to walk out of their portals. The light surrounding the wives and their pleasant smell woke the rest of the Lords. Cade noticed that Clave did not wake up immediately and flew over to wake him. Cade grabbed Clave's jaws and stretched them out of shape. Clave then immediately woke up and playfully placed Cade in a headlock.

Nicolette sighed out of embarrassment, "Why do they have to act so facetious on such a day?"

Nicolette then summoned a strong wind forcing them to the ground.

The two, laughing hysterically, helped each other up. As they looked over at their wives, their jaws dropped.

"Stunning," said Clave.

"Oh-yeah!" Cade agreed.

The wives decorated themselves in beautiful gold earrings and wore diamond crowns, bracelets, and necklaces. They wore makeup and decorated their nails in diamond liquid and gold polish. All of the wives were astonished by their own enhancements while giving praise and thanks to Zuccaro and Nefertari.

"I guess it's your turn, Clave! Saving the best for last!" said Cade excitedly.

With a twinkle in his eye, Clave responded, "You betcha!"

Clave had the biggest smile on his face as he approached his wife and sisters.

"Like our brother Jireh, I got a vision from the clouds. One day I awoke from my temple and my entire temple was filled with clouds. I thought it was a joke from Cade, but I soon realized that the clouds had simply hovered over the land that day. Rather than raising the clouds back to the skies, I kept them there. I found the clouds to be relaxing and pleasing on my skin. So, I lounged within them as I pondered the gift I wanted to present to our wives. I then took notice of one smaller cloud. The shape immediately grabbed my attention. I sat on the floor and pulled the cloud closer to view its shape. It had a body with four legs: even a head with two ears attached like ours. I thought it was rather interesting, but slightly annoying as well. As I floated throughout my temple it seemed to follow me as well. I felt like it was bound to me. This small and insignificant thing did not care about who I was, yet it clinged to me. I decided to test this theory in the simplest way. I got up and bounced in the clouds and it too bounced there as well. I played with this loyal cloud all day! I then noticed that it began to evaporate but I wasn't ready for it to go! I gave it the name Khan and kept it whole. I then gathered Khan and nine others clouds and formed them for this very day... for another life to come forth," Clave explained.

"You decided to give life to these clouds because it made you happy? Would now be the correct time to create such a thing? There must be more to this," Nicolette probed.

Clave took his box and made it ascend to the ALL Power and said, "Yes, there is more." He then continued to say, "when I am with one or two of you, I am happy. But when all ten of us are together I feel at home, and I feel the loyalty."

About thirty minutes later, ten small beings withdrew from the All Power. Both the Lords and their wives could hear them barking and howling with joy.

"What language is this?" questioned Genus.

With tears in his eyes, Clave said, "Their language. Listen to their hearts, brother. They are praising the All Power even now." Clave reached up and said, "Khan! Come here, boy!" The small being heard its master and opened the wings on its back and descended to him with full speed.

"I truly do believe our wives and offspring will bring something new to our lives. Hence, my gift is loyalty. It is important to me that you see and experience this as I did. These additions will be a blessing for each of you. Behold!" said Clave. The puppy Khan flew into Clave's arms and started to lick him nonstop. Khan resembled a husky breed of dog. He was covered in a light brown coat with the left eye being light blue and the right eye green.

Clave was tickled and laughed non-stop from the puppy's constant affection.

"Clio Clave, call him to you! He is yours," said Clave

Clio Clave smiled and said, "He's so cute! Alright then! Come here boy!" Khan didn't hesitate and flew into Clio's arms. Clio held Khan up and said, "and with such beautiful eyes! Thank you, Clave! I love him." Clave blushed and bowed his head.

Cade looked up and said, "Why aren't the rest of the Khans coming down?"

"Haha! Khan is the name of *my* dog. Give your dog a name and it will come to you," said Clave.

"So, they're called dogs? Interesting name choice," said Genus.

The Lords began to call each of their dogs one by one.

"Cerberus! Come here," said Genesi in a stern voice.

Jireh stood with his wife and held her hand as they watched everyone play with their dogs. Velandris Jireh looked at her husband and smiled.

"Jireh, all have called on their dogs except for you. Tell me, is something the matter?" asked Velandris.

Jireh then looked into Velandris's eyes and said, I'm just taking it all in. You. Everyone. I'm overwhelmed with happiness. I'm filled with joy to finally meet you and see everyone elated. Velandris smiled and placed her arms around him and said, "I'm happy to be here too. Thank you, Jireh." Her words of gratitude filled him. Jireh took a strong notice of these foreign emotions within him. They completely overtook him, and his heart melted. "I feel extremely overwhelmed and find it very difficult to think. Jireh took in this moment and opened his heart to Velandris and decided that he will assess these emotions another day.

"Velandris, everyone seems to be waiting on us. Would you do us the honor and name our dog?" asked Jireh. Velandris smiled and began floating. She folded her legs like a pretzel as did her husband. As Velandris began to think, she placed her hand on her chin and looked to the clouds. The Lords were astonished. "Well look at that! Velandris looks just like Jireh when he's thinking," Genus said.

Jireh smiled and rubbed the back of her head. "I got it!" she said excitedly.

Velandris yelled out, "Karama! Come here boy!" Karama heard the voice of his master and howled at the All Power. He opened his small wings and darted towards Velandris howling right into her arms. Karama was full of excitement and energy and fought to get out of Velandris' arms just to shower her with a barrage of kisses.

"He's a feisty one," said Cenci.

Jireh and Velandris both laughed as they rubbed and played with their new puppy. Karama resembled a cloud storm cloaked in all white with wavy hair and lightening eyes the color of amethyst. The tip of Karama's tail and paws were engulfed in purple flames. "Jireh, Velandris Jireh, Karama's flames will never harm the ones that he loves. You all should know that your dog can grow to incredible size. All you have to do is command it to do so," said Clave.

Jireh commented, "these dogs will make great additions to our new families."

They stayed there for another hour and gave thanks as they prepared to go. Genesi approached his wife and said, "Adrielle, you were created to please me. So tell me, what do you know about creation? Adrielle gracefully placed her hand on the side of his face gazing into his eyes. She then slid her hand all the way down to his penis and said, "that you don't know the first thing about it. Of this, I am one-hundred percent sure." Genesi was shocked by her words. "After you show me around my new home I will show you what real creation is," said Adrielle seductively. For the first time in Genesi's life, he felt vulnerable and was at a loss for words. He was extremely impressed by her crafty words and thought process. She then grabbed both of his hands and pulled him closer to her.

"What's the matter? Are you not pleased with me?" asked Adrielle.

He quickly answered, "By design, we are made to be attracted to one another. The probability..."

Adrielle silenced Genesi by quickly leaning in and kissing him on the lips. Genesi was stunned. His thought process immediately faded away. The soft-touch of her lips made Genesi lose all power and ultimately let his guard down. It caused Genesi to truly take an interest in his wife. Adrielle smiled and said in a demanding tone, "We have much to do. Let us go at once!"

"Fine, let us take our leave," Genesi agreed.

Genesi then looked down at Cerberus and noticed how calm he was. "He's Intrigued by you. It seems that he enjoys watching and learning," said Adrielle. Cerberus then stood up and sat down in front of his masters. "Our Cerberus is wise, on guard, and saving his energy," said Adrielle.

Genesi looked down at Cerberus and said, "You will be greater than the rest of them."

CHAPTER 7
The Holy Spirit Arrives

Before leaving Mount Olympus, the Lords and their wives formed a circle one final time to praise the All Power. Strangely, their puppies began to bark and howl at the All Power creating a lack of focus in the Lord's worship. Nicolette, now visibly frustrated, asked, "Clave, why are these dogs being so rude? Tell us how to calm them down."

Clave examined the dogs using their heartbeats and immediately was met with uneasiness and perplexation.

"One trait that I placed in these dogs was a good sense of awareness. Although we know the shift and time of things because we made them, they know the change in the spirit before we notice them. These dogs are able to look past the heart and pick up on patterns," said Clave.

Clave then took his eyes off the dogs and looked at his brothers with concern and realized that they weren't barking or howling at the All Power. Looking up at the All Power as well, Clave felt an eerie chill run down his back. "Your dogs are made to love and to protect you. Always listen to your dog, brothers. They aren't being rude but simply doing their job. They are trying to provide information," said Clave.

A drastic shift in the atmosphere immediately occurred. The Lords stood to their feet and faced the All Power. With a lump in his throat, Kian Kiani pushed out the question, "What are these strange vibrations emitting from the All Power?"

Unexpectedly, their world started to shake, and a gush of wind swept around them. The All Power then grew and imprinted itself again into their reality with a flash of light. An image of itself hoovered around the All Power. This new layer of the All Power retracted back to its normal size, emitting a brighter light than before. The light was so great that even the Lords could not look onto it, except for Jireh. They tried to command the winds to cease, and for heaven to stop shaking, but their efforts were useless. Their power began to be siphoned from them, because the All Power had become weakened. Genesi looked at his hands in disbelief as he felt a sharp decrease in his strength.

The Lord's tried to grab and pull back their power, but the All Power overtook them and demanded its power from them.

"What is happening to me?" yelled Genesi.

"My power, I can't hold on to it!" cried Cenci.

Everyone panicked as Jireh stood there with his eyes glowing staring up at the All Power. He was stunned but had the strength to stand through it all. "How is this possible?" he said.

Jireh saw two All Powers, with a smaller one within the All Power. Jireh then understood what he was able to see. The original All Power had produced another image. The birth of the new image was a devastating experience for the Lords and for reality itself, because nothing was stable. The power and energy that came from the All Power started disfiguring and warping all Heaven and reality. Its power expanded, reaching to every corner of their universe. The inner image then began to transform, taking the shape of a body. This caused the world to stop shaking instantly allowing normalcy to return. The body then free fell from the All Power; Zuccaro and Nefertari took notice and linked their minds together. They sensed a foreign energy from the falling body, an energy that shook them at their core. It frightened them, so they became hostile and exploded with rage and fury.

"Whatever that thing is, it's stealing our power! It must GO NOW!" yelled Nefertari.

"Indeed, it must be destroyed," Zuccaro agreed.

"We'll rip it apart!" the two said in unison.

Prior to this moment, death was an irrelevant topic since everything was made to live forever. However, the dethroning of their power made each of them consider this new possibility.

The rest of the Lords were startled by Zuccaro and Nefertari's bizarre behavior. Genesi was now able to see the raw body falling as well. Genesi then heard the groanings of his twin brothers and looked at them. He saw that they were about to attack the foreign object. Genesi screamed, "Take no part in it, you fools! That creature is in the rawest form of energy. That type of light and power may actually kill you."

However, Zuccaro and Nefertari did not heed Genesi's words because they were too fixated on the falling body. Blood then ran from both Zuccaro and Nefertari's eyes as they shrieked and pulled at the roots of their hair. Falling to their knees, they began to ram their heads into the ground. Their wives tried to help them, but the twin Lord's ordered them away.

The other brothers were confused and were shocked as they listened to the twin Lord's manic laugh.

"What has happened? What is wrong with them?" said Nicolette.

The twin Lords were unusually weary as tears and blood dripped from their faces.

"Make it stop! But it feels so good!" They said in unison.

Genesi smirked, then glared at them, "They are defective!"

Cenci turned and yelled at Genesi, "You be quiet! I've had enough of your negativity today."

"Jireh! What shall we do?" asked Clave.

Just as Jireh was about to speak, Zuccaro and Nefertari stood up and said, "We will destroy that light!" They then took flight towards the falling body.

"No! You mustn't," yelled Jireh.

"I don't know what that light is, but if it comes from the All Power then it is good. However, Genesi is right. That type of energy is foreign to us, I need to protect that light and my brothers," Jireh thought. He continued, "you all will kneel down and praise the All Power while I stop our wayward brothers."

Jireh then took off at max speed, while knocking everyone down due to the force of his sudden launch.

As Jireh flew past the clouds, he began to worry about his brother's state of mind. What has happened to them? Why would they want to destroy any-thing that comes from the All Power? More impor-tantly why is the All Power reacting in such a way," he thought.

Zuccaro and Nefertari looked back and saw Jireh trailing them and said, "We knew you would come... we know that you feel it as well. You feel life in that Light!"

Jireh cried out, "Do not touch that Light!"

"You do not command us!" they responded. "That Light... It will change everything! Everything that we have worked for! Go back Jireh," they ordered.

Jireh shook his head and yelled out, "The All Power does not serve us! It is we that serve the All Power! That Light is part of its will! You must not destroy anything that it has created!"

Still, the two did not waiver or listen. "Stopping those two alone will be difficult," he thought. Jireh reached out his hand and tried to weld reality with hopes of stopping them but he failed. He was bewil-dered as to why he was no longer able to command reality anymore. As he flew through the clouds, Zuccaro and Nefertari were but a few seconds from reaching the falling Light. Jireh then summoned an incredible amount of energy in his hands.

"If I can muster up enough power to force them away, I'll have an advantage. It won't stop them, but it just might delay them, and I am quickly running out of time," Jireh thought.

The twin Lord's sensed Jireh approaching fast. The deranged twins looked back at Jireh and summoned two small suns from their hands, that were twice the size of their bodies. As they reached back to launch their attack. Jireh heard his name being yelled from below him.

"Jireh! Move my love!"

Jireh did as instructed as a burst from the clouds gave way to two powerful force waves that flew past him. The waves connected with Zuccaro and Nefertari, pushing them past the falling Light and in disarray. Their two suns collided causing a massive explosion that launched Zuccaro and Nefertari across the land and in the opposite direction of one another. Jireh looked behind him to see Velandris tailing him. "Velandris!" Jireh yelled with excitement. Jireh took advantage of his wife's help and caught the falling Light. As Jireh held the Light in his arms, it immediately blessed him with power, then the Light returned to the All Power. Jireh was instantly filled with joy and knew that this power was good.

Velandris asked, "Jireh, are you ok?" Realizing that he was still holding something, Velandris saw the long black hair flowing in the wind. Jireh watched as the Light reentered the All Power and slowly blinked his eyes in awe. Shaking, he kept his eyes on the All Power wondering if something would happen next.

"Jireh, look!" Velandris ordered.

Jireh, startled by Verandris's shock, looked at the body, and said, "What in all creation? It's a female Lord!"

CHAPTER 8
A Sacrifice

The heavens had finally returned to its original calm and quiet state after the commotion. The chaos from the winds had died down. Everything seemed to be stable and back to normal as Jireh and Velandris descended from the clouds landing near the rest of the Lords. They collectively felt weaker than before and questioned their abilities. Jireh, shaken up by everything that happened yelled, "Go! Go to them! Retrieve our brothers!" At this point, Jireh is visibly trembling and distraught. His hands quivered uncontrollably as he held onto the lifeless body in his arms. Velandris was deeply concerned for her husband and took the lifeless body from him saying, "Husband, sit down and rest. I'll take it from here. Nefertari is to the east of us, Zuccaro to the west. Please attend to them."

"Of course! We're on our way! Come Clio and Crusuis," said Clave. The two wives followed him and took off in search of Zuccaro. "Come Hera, Kalmali you as well. We'll find Nefertari," said Cenci. They all took flight and headed east.

Kian Kiani, Cade, Genus and Nicolette did not waste any time running over to Jireh while Genesi slowly walked over to Velandris. Keeping an eye on the lifeless body, Genesi asked, "Was there a miscalculation? I counted ten yet there are eleven. Jireh, Cade, Nicolette- explain this mistake." They all turned and looked at Genesi. Nicolette spoke first saying, "There were no mistakes made brother."

Cade quickly followed, "He's right brother, we only sent ten."

"I find it hard to believe anything coming from a facetious tongue!" said Genesi.

Genesi asked Velandris to lay the body down and step back. Kneeling, Genesi began to examine the body. He lifted her eyelids to find her eye sockets empty and no sign of a brain. He noticed how cold her body was and placed his hands over her head in hopes of communicating with her soul. Ten minutes went by only to conclude that the female Lord was nothing but an empty shell. "There is nothing in here!

No sign of life whatsoever!" said Genesi as he stood up and faced his brothers.

"It seems that you have miscalculated, Jireh. Zuccaro and Nefertari's senses are stronger when they are in unison. They sensed the danger long before we did. This was the reason they lost sight of themselves. I blame this abomination because this curse has weakened us! The light in us is gone and has returned to the All Power. Even our wives lost what little they had. We're nowhere near as powerful as we were! You should have let the twin Lords destroy it! I'm sure it would have stopped the occurrence altogether," said Genesi.

"Power, is that all that you care about? If the All Power chooses to rescind power, then it is for a reason! Let it take! As long as we're together, that's all that matters!" said Genus.

Kian Kiani slowly helped Jireh to his feet. Though he was still drained and exhausted, Jireh appeared more frightened than anyone as his hands continued to shake. Trying to regain his composure, he thought, what has happened to me? This is such an intense feeling. He began to speak aloud, "We are beings of light and peace; beings born to explore and learn. That body came from the All Power, destroying it was not the answer. It was not for us to do. I believe it was given to us for a reason."

Genesi disagreed with Jireh's response, so he lifted the lifeless body off the ground with his power for all to see. He then pointed at the corpse. "This thing is clearly a mistake from the All Power. It re-imaged a body without instructions. This spirit has no life, no soul, no intelligence implemented whatsoever! It has cursed us, striping control over our own world, over our own reality!" With all his anger, might, and power, Genesi furiously rammed the lifeless body through the mountains and into a deep underground temple they built years ago.

"Trash!" Genesi yelled.

Genesi then turned and looked at Jireh, "Foolish Provider, if you couldn't tell by now, you are significantly weaker than us. Just look at yourself, stupidly acting without hesitation or proper thought. You held that light in its rawest form, now look at you!"

Jireh's skin had turned sky blue opposed to his normal deep-sea blue.

"Tell me, Great Provider. How does it feel to lose most of your power, the very thing that made you equal to us?" Genesi's words hurt, and Jireh lowered his head, unresponsive.

"If you were wise, you'd let our monotonous brothers take that risk," Genesi continued. All ten were stunned by Genesi's words yet said nothing.

Cade, seeing Jireh in distress stepped in front of him saying, "That is enough! Can't you see that he's already down?"

Genesi was shocked by Cade's response and responded sarcastically, "Apparently you do have a serious side."

"Now is not the time to be irate! We need to figure out what's going on," Kian Kiani reasoned.

Genus placed his glasses further onto his face and began to walk back and forth. "Yes, Kiani is correct. Let us take our focus away from this topic for now. But I will say this, Jireh had good intentions whether you disagree with him or not. Let us not shame what is good."

Velandris got up and grabbed Jireh's face and looked into his eyes and said, "My Husband, do not look so sad. You are too beautiful to do so. You believed that you were doing the right thing, protecting everything dear to you. All can see the good in you and if you have acted foolishly, then I will be a fool with you. We will suffer together."

"Even at the risk of bringing shame?" Jireh asked.

Velandris smiled, reassuring him. "Shame, there is none, but if there is, I'll follow you again. I'd gladly take half of the shame." Jireh was shocked by her words and said "Encouraging and brave. You have not lived a full day and yet you are full of kindness and love. Thank you, Velandris."

Pushing his glasses up once more, Genus stepped in and said, "Pardon me for my sudden inclusion, but I believe that I may have an answer to our problem. How should I put this? I believe with the proper amount of mana, we may be able to restore some of our power. However, we would need to eat it daily to maintain our strength to perform. I also believe by syncing with one another more often, we may be able to transfer power thus balancing one another like in the past."

Nicolette then chimed in, "I'm in agreement. Mana does give us a bit of a refreshing boost. Back when we were truly one mind, we were the same, correct? As of now, we act and think as our own entities which I believe has diluted our current synchronization. Personally speaking, becoming one has gotten to be rather difficult. Our connection has had more inactivity than usual which explains the poor syncing. We have stopped learning from one another and pursued ourselves. I highly doubt that we can become one body and one mind being that we are individuals now. I began pondering if we've done something wrong, and questioned if we're still walking the correct path?"

"Meaning if we should have continued moving as one rather than separating?" asked Cade.

"Precisely," Nicolette responded.

Genesi stepped in and began speaking, "This is senseless thinking Nicolette. You and I both know that this was inevitable. It was bound to happen much like our births. Our very births tell the natural way of things. All networks will malfunction over time after it masters its route and there will be wear and tear at some point. It only took one drop of communication for it all to crash and for us to realize our own existence."

"There may be truth in that, but ultimately, it was a choice that we made. We may be the second drop of communication. Though it is an unfortunate loss, I believe it's a necessary one after assessing the matter," Nicolette sternly noted.

Jireh looked at Nicolette and said, "Necessary? What are you proposing, brother?"

Nicolette looked at the All Power grimly and said, "A sacrifice of self." He then turned and looked at his brothers saying, "We would need to utterly destroy who we are in order to accomplish this."

Immediately taken back by Nicolette's words, Genesi replied, "This is impossible. The spirit design is eternal."

"I am not speaking of the spirit, but the soul! The sphere only carries our personalities and the static from the cloud allows us to sync with one another. I'm proposing a new covenant. We remove the old cloud so that our soul may recreate a new one," Nicolette suggested.

Pushing his glasses upright, Genus began, "There is truth in what our brother's words. However, all our souls must be in alignment with this. All must be pure at heart in wanting this to happen. We cannot form a cloud within us if there isn't a desire first. Genesi, if we are all in agreement with this, what is the success rate for this exchange?"

"Hardly any," Genesi replied. "We are all separate beings now. It's not ideal that we take this course. But if I have to generate a number... I'd say there is about twenty to thirty percent for success."

Cade cried out in frustration then fell face first to the ground yelling out in grief.

"Cade calm down, it's just a thought," said Nicolette.

"A thought that became a word!" yelled Cade as he slowly raised his head. "The concept of losing my humor is horrible! But I guess if it helps the situation, I'll sacrifice it. Besides, our wives are part of who we are now. We can look to them and remember some of our old characteristics."

"Yes brother, that is correct," said Genus.

Jireh began, "I am in full agreement. Sacrificing ourselves to be one mind just might please the All Power. It could mean a true restoration of balance and control. If we all come to the same consensus then I would also suggest that we get to know one another again," he continued, "We ought to live in the temple below us and gain nourishment from the All Power. With the added strength from the mana and each other, we could be on one accord much sooner than we think."

"Perhaps now would be the correct time for me to speak. Please hear me. I'm not against this, but I am for our success. I, myself have been questioning a number of things that I must find the answers to. Before doing anything, I must find peace with my thoughts," Kian Kiani said.

Clave looked at Kian Kiani and said, "Tell us about the stronghold that is blocking you from moving forward? We may be able to provide answers for you to crush your thoughts."

Kian Kiani nodded his head. "Very well. I still contemplate our existence and the things that we claim to be our true purpose. From the beginning, I either agreed or disagreed with our flow of thinking and never questioned anything. And now that I'm fully aware, this situation gnaws at me from within. You mentioned, 'correct path'. Tell me, what is the 'correct path'? Most importantly, who suggested this path? The All Power created us but does not speak to us, which leads me to believe that we took it upon ourselves and believed that we're its conscious. I now believe that this truth could be false," said Kian Kiani.

"That's blasphemy Kiani!" An angry Genesi spewed back. "You and your reckless words have gone too far this time. Must I remind you that we are the product of our creator! Thus we are creators by default. It would be wise for you to remove this foolishness from your heart."

"And if I do not?" Kian Kiani looked at Genesi with sternness. Kian Kiani then continued, "It would be wise for everyone to listen, especially you Genesi. You are clearly the most intelligent, yet the most single minded of us all. You only see one way! One answer, and that's your flaw... brother. The question that I presented needs to be addressed so that we may have a full understanding before making a final decision. Then may we be in true alignment and in true unison."

"You have drifted so far away. Never have I stopped what we have started. As for you, your level of thinking is unacceptable, and I question who you are becoming! You should repent! Your thoughts are extremely dangerous and obviously corrupt. It violates our order and curses the mind of all who are listening. Yes, we must now take the proper steps in restoring order, because you and some of the other brothers are defective!" said Genesi.

"Defective? I think not! I know you well, and you know me. Can't you see that there is something missing, that we don't have true guidance? If that is the case, then allow me to fix your blurry vision by removing the dirt from your eyes. I don't care if we go backward or forward as long as we can agree and confess these hidden thoughts. We should then seek our purpose from the All Power. But to leave this personality of mine to share one mind for the sake of restoring our power is futile. A balance of power should not drive us to do anything. Learning the true origins of ourselves and the All Power should always be our goal. Trying to figure out our real reason for life, again, needs to be reevaluated. I say that there should be no sacrifices from us at this time," Kian Kiani argued.

Genesi began to speak up, "Kian... Kiani. The answer you seek is right in front of you. It is our desires from within that pushes us forward. We all carry the answers, that's why we're together! We need the power of the All Power to keep going further! To maintain purpose! So that we may have an answer to your ridiculous thoughts."

"You simply enjoy the control," Kian Kiani snapped back. "But you have no control. We are together but we are not one. Even Jireh's declaration showed us this. We are becoming null. Hence, the suggestion that we live together again. We lack understanding of who we have become at this point. We shouldn't even consider ourselves to be the consciousness of the All Power because we are not the same anymore. Even our traditions are dwindling away. Outside of our wives, are there any real reasons to do what we've been doing at this point? Especially when there is no clear depiction of what our purpose is?"

"I've had enough of this! There will be no more from you, Kiani!" yelled Genesi.

Kian Kiani was angered, rising with power. "NO! You do not command me! You only command yourself! When we were one mind and linked with the All Power, was it our own thinking or was it the All Power that told us to create? Was it? If not! A desire had to come first before a thought, and after a thought, a word, then a mission. There is no clear proof that the All Power commanded the ten of us to create!"

Kian Kiani's wife then grabbed her husband, calming him down.

Genus offering his take on the situation said, "It is rather an interesting theory and admittedly, I have thought of it at least once and from that theory came these questions. What if there was another voice? Rather, what if there was something coded within us that brought on the desire to create? We naturally agreed to the order of creation but there seemed to be no other choice other than to create."

"I cannot disagree, but since then we have evolved. At this point, have we not done everything? Now is the time to seek a greater understanding and purpose outside of creating offspring. There is nothing more that we desire then to create so we need to raise the question of why and what now? There is no clear-cut answer, but there should be. None of us have been given the answers or authority in which we should follow. We have created our own paths and established our way. Taking the chance and destroying who we are because of these unanswered theories is not the way, especially now that we have wives. Destroying our personalities would be a disadvantage to them and their absolute purpose," said Kian Kiani.

"You talk and complain so much!" Genesi yelled, "You have literally become hollow! You talk in circles yet add nothing of value Kiani! The fact is, we need a solution to regain our power. Your thoughts and questions are secondary."

"Fine, then consider this a solution. Let us keep our bodies and raise our offspring to restore us and answer our deepest questions," suggested Kian Kiani. He continued, "Raise them to be like us, and to obey us. We will take the best of the ten and rank them from least to greatest. Once they are mature, we will vote for the worthiest offspring to sacrifice. Let us create a device that will connect the soul to the All Power. That offspring will be commanded to restore order to us so that we may seek the depths of ourselves and discover our purpose."

Shocked by Kian Kiani's solution, the other nine brothers unanimously disagreed. "No!" Jireh yelled. "We can't do that! Your suggestion is extremely dangerous and beyond us all."

Painfully, Genus spoke, "I agree with Jireh. Having all that power could be a danger to us. How could we trust that the offspring will restore us? He or she could change their mind once consumed."

Immediately struck with an idea, Genesi pretended to disagree and said, "Though it might be a horrible idea, it is not impossible. This could be successful by making sure that it does not develop a personality. It will only operate from its sub-conscious which we can program." Hearing Genesi's idea, the Lords began to open up to the suggestion that this just might be possible. All but Jireh shook his head saying, "This is cruel Genesi. There has to be another way."

Genesi quickly responded, "As much as I hate to say this, I am at peace with Kiani's idea, a sacrifice is the only way!"

The Lords knew that by sacrificing their souls to the All power that they would lose their individual identities and would never be the same. Though their wives would be an image of their former selves, the Lord's loved who they had become. Their original way of thinking had become a distant memory. Though they would be restored to power, their new identities would be lost. It was then that Genus pushed his glasses closer to face and stepped forward.

However, before Genus spoke, Cenci stepped in, "We should just sacrifice our souls and have our wives reteach us our personalities. It would be a long process, but this is the most promising way to restore ourselves, and learn from our mistakes."

Frustrated Genesi said, "For us to be back to our original state of mind would take eons! It would take half of our life span to return back to our current state of mind even with the help of our wives. I agree with Kiani's idea."

Genus then stepped forward and said, "Brothers, we have a sacrifice. As much as I don't like this idea. It would be best that we move forward, Jireh."

Jireh began chiming in but Genus continued his sentiment. "Listen, I choose not to use our offspring for our own selfish gain. I know that if the ten of us were to go up, then we would only die to our current selves, But, if the ten of us who are solid could stand in agreement, we could balance the power once we are up there and our souls would not be truly destroyed. This is how we would return to our spirit bodies. But if one were to go, then the power would ultimately overtake the one soul and destroy it. The chosen vessel would only have a short period of time to restore us. I've come to this, if we can make sure that our success rate is one hundred percent, then I'll go, I'll sacrifice my soul and restore my brothers."

CHAPTER 9
The Holy Spirit

Genus' suggestion to sacrifice himself, put an unprecedented damper on everyone's mood. Even his wife wanted to disagree with the proposed plan, but she knew that this decision was for the best; instead she chose to keep silent and grabbed his hand in support of his decision. A sudden stream of outbursts from the other Lords interrupted the tender moment shared between Genus and his wife.

"Out of the question!" said Cenci.

Nicolette concurred, "I will not allow it!"

"That's not funny, Genus! Think about your wife! Think about us!" yelled Cade.

"I have! Don't you all trust me? And as for my wife... she's just like me. She understands that this is for the greater good," Genus explained.

The greater good? Jireh thought.

"Genus, you're so intelligent. Even with all my insight, I still don't want this for you. It must be an offspring," Genesi insisted.

"I'm flattered that you care, but I won't be gone. I'm simply returning to where I came from," Genus answered.

It had been a while since Kian Kiani spoke after a deep pondering. He finally offered an opinion on Genus' suggestion. "As much as I love our brother and hate saying this; I believe that this is the best route. I feel that Genus is the best candidate to present as a sacrifice. He is the most well rounded of us and has been the fastest one to resolve our most difficult obstacles. He's not too far right or too far left when opinionated and he's a good mix of all our personalities."

Jireh and Cade went over to Genus and embraced him. "Brother, I implore you to see reason and reconsider," said Cade as he released Genus from the hug. Genus closed his eyes and lowered his head, "I'm sorry, Cade... Jireh, but It only makes sense that I do this," said Genus.

"Genus, I am content with who and what we are now. Like all other challenges we've faced, we always figure out the best solution. Wait brother, let us think as we always have...as one," Jireh pleaded.

"Trust me brother, this is the best option. If we can secure my mind just long enough before my mind is destroyed, I can surely restore you. It will be worth it," said Genus.

Uneased and frustrated with Genus' words, Jireh shouted, "Very well! If this is what you all want, a sacrifice for power...that is your decision, not mine!"

With tears in his eyes Cade yelled, "No, Brothers! We have to make sure that his mind doesn't dissolve!"

"Get a hold of yourselves!" Genesi began. "Nothing is impossible for us. We will be successful regardless of the outcome. We will be restored and complete our mission."

Disgusted at his brother's nonchalant attitude, Cade responded, "You speak so casually about this, as if you don't care! This is our brother! My brother."

Jireh in agreement said, "This is no small thing. There has to be another way!"

Cade quickly responded, "If we cannot preserve his mind then...I'm..."

"What Cade? Out?" Genesi questioned. "If you're not for our overall advancement then what is your purpose? Why are you here? I too do not wish this for Genus, but it is his choice! And I trust him enough to do as he says."

Cade glared at Genesi saying, "I've had enough of this. When I can't grin or think of something amusing, well... It makes me sick. And if you haven't noticed, this is sickening! Let us put the matter to bed for the day."

Picking up his dog, Cade began walking away. "My wife and I will take our leave now. Let me know when there is a real proposition."

The remaining brothers were taken back by Cade's assertiveness. They've yet to experience Cade this upset.

Jireh sighed heavily, "I for one agree... That would be best for now."

"I agree. Let us drop it... for now," Kian Kiani said to his brothers.

"So be it," said Genesi.

Genus offered a plan as a way to ease the tension between him and his brothers. "Tomorrow we will go and analyze Zuccaro and Nefertari. Let's hope that their damages aren't too troubling."

Agreeing, the brothers said their farewells, took flight and flew away. Velandris and Jireh stayed behind and watched the other Lord's ascension. He began to weep as he looked off into the distance as he thought about the events that transpired over the course of the day. He looked down and noticed Karama fast asleep and smiled at the innocence displayed. That moment led him to find the beauty in everything that happened and ultimately thanked the All Power. He picked Karama up and walked to the edge of the mountain. Looking up at the All power, he questioned, "What has become of us? It seems that change was inevitable from the beginning."

Velandris slowly walked up to Jireh, grabbing Karama, and placed him in the pocket of Jireh's robe. She grabbed his hand and said, "Then let change come. We'll face it together."

Surprised by her response, Jireh turned and faced his wife. "Your words and your eyes reflect one another. Not only are they beautiful, but they are also comforting," Jireh said lovingly. She smiled and nodded her head at Jireh with equal adoration.

"This day was supposed to be a day of celebration, but it turned out to be the very opposite. Velandris, I am sorry. You and our sisters have seen the wrong side of us. Please, do not let today's events move you. Though you were born with wisdom, you have yet to experience anything. However, I am honored and happy that you are here; that moving forward I can experience everything with you," he said.

Velandris responded by pulling Jireh closer to her and rested her head on his chest. "Thank you for creating me. I am fully aware and happy to serve you, as your purpose has now become mine. May I serve you forever and bring you joy."

Jireh felt Velandris' loving nature which comforted him further. She looked him in the eyes and placed her soft hand gently on the side of his face. She reached up using the tips of her toes while closing her eyes, pulled him closer and kissed him on the lips. Jireh's golden eyes lit up in awe as he felt his heart race like never before. His mind had become completely at ease as he focused on the feeling of her lips against his and the flow of the windy breeze.

He slowly broke away from her lips and immediately smiled. "That was amazing," he said with a slight giggle.

Velandris chuckled too, "Yes, it was very nice."

"I'll never let go of your hand," Jireh said.

"Don't," she replied.

Jireh picked her up and held her in his arms as they levitated off the ground. They smiled at one another and kissed again.

"Are we going to your temple now? She asked.

"No, we are going to our temple. But first there is something that we have to do," he said

Jireh flew over to the hole Genesi created with the lifeless body that came from the All Power.

He gradually flew down the hole in search of the missing cadaver.

"Velandris, there is something that I must tell you," Jireh began. "When I held the body in my arms, there was a living light within it. I felt some of that light enter me at the moment the light left her body and my skin color changed to this lighter color. I felt weakened like my brothers, but that light that entered me...I can still feel it. It's subtle and I don't feel as weak as before."

"As before? Do you believe that this light is restoring your power?" Velandris asked.

"It's too early to say, but I am not as weak as my brother," he replied.

"Why didn't you tell the others? Perhaps that light is the solution for us all. Maybe the solution is within you. We could possibly even avoid a sacrifice from Lord Genus," she said.

"Genus is always the first one to implement a solution. He is quick to think and quick on his feet. In this case, he wants to be the solution. The All Power alone would be too much for him to handle. Myself, Genesi, Genus, and Cade knew that he would die. He believes it's for the greater good. I believe with patience and with time, we can figure out a better resolution but for now, I must analyze myself and protect that body that came from the All Power," said Jireh.

"I see..." she responded.

Jireh went on, "Also, Netertari and Zuccaro's sudden outburst has worried us. I don't believe that it was the body that triggered them. Rather the light that the body held. That's why for now, we must not tell them about me. I don't even understand it."

Velandris agreed, "Yes, we should all rest and clear our heads."

"Indeed, rest is needed. Besides, I believe that Genesi would feel uneasy if he knew I were stronger than him. We must maintain peace and harmony amongst all the Lords," said Jireh.

Velandris nodded in agreement with her husband's sentiments.

Jireh landed at the bottom of the mountain and into their temple of worship. He set Velandris down and they both began their search for the abandoned body. As they removed rocks and boulders with their power, Velandris asked, "Is Genesi always that angry?"

Jireh sighed, "Only when he doesn't get what he wants. He is the youngest of us all. It's safe to say that we spoiled him."

"A little too much I'd say," said Velandris.

"Unfortunately... The truth is, he built his temple the furthest from the All Power. Ever since then, he changed for the worse," he explained.

As soon as Jireh finished speaking, Velandris noticed a hand sticking out among the rubble.

"Jireh! There!" she said with excitement.

Jireh quickly grabbed Velandris' hand and flew over to the body. With a wave of his hand, the rock covering the body was removed. Shocked to see her body, Velandris quickly picked her up.

"Her skin, it has changed to the same color as yours," Velandris said puzzled.

"This is strange!" he replied.

Velandris took her and laid her down in the sunshine. Jireh examined her and could not find anything out of the ordinary. She was constructed the same as the rest of the Lords and Female Lords.

"There is nothing wrong with her body but a lock of her hair has broken off somewhere," he said.

"Probably from the damages," Velandris replied.

"Likely so... but I'm still pondering. Why did the All Power make a replica of the female body?" questioned Jireh.

Jireh and Velandris both started to levitate. Crossing their legs and began to brainstorm. After an hour of exchanging their ideas with one another, they both agreed that none of their theories could be proven.

"Then what shall we do with her? We can't just leave her here," said Velandris.

"Beneath the temple is a storage room... well a room that we had planned for storage. We'll place her down there for now," said Jireh.

Velandris questioned the proposed option immediately, "A storage room? I thought you wanted to protect her?"

Jireh picked up the body, "I am, follow me."

The tunnel they began down was dark with only specs of light on the walls. Eventually, they passed an invisible barrier as they neared the end of the tunnel leading them to a cliff. Beneath the cliff glowed a great light, where golden auras lit the altar below.

Velandris looked around and noticed a shift. "Jireh, the atmosphere changed drastically. Are we not underneath Mount Olympus anymore?"

"We are," he replied. "This realm is the subspace of Heaven. It has a sky and clouds just like our home... but this world is used for storage... its massive world of storage."

A world of storage. What do you call this place?" she asked.

"It is called the Solaris of Infinite Space. It is a parallel world to our own," he answered.

"The Solaris? What were you and your brothers planning to store down here?" asked Velandris.

"Maybe a few solar systems and other postponed projects," Jireh said.

"I see! Look at that. The golden floor... is it... moving?" Velandris asked.

"That is not a floor, but an ocean of living water. An ocean of no end. There is none like it. You see, whatever is placed in it will be preserved and if left in the water long enough; a diamond case will form around the object and keep it sealed forever," he expounded.

Jireh then looked at Velandris, "Come, jump with me."

Jireh smiled at her and jumped off the edge with the lifeless spirit being held in his left arm. Velandris did not hesitate, jumping seconds after him. They broke through the sky of the Solaris.

"It will take a bit of time before we reach the destination. We will free fall for a few minutes and then we shall arrive," Jireh said, reaching back grabbing Velandris' hand. "The clouds will soon form beneath us and become a platform. Then I'll lower this lifeless body into the water."

They descended for about ten minutes until clouds formed underneath their feet and reduced the speed of their fall. The cloud took hold of them and lowered them to the surface of the golden sea, Jireh said, "I suppose this is it for now, hollowed one."

Velandris looked upon her regrettably, "I wish there were more that we could do for her." She continued, "She is beautiful, is she not Jireh?"

"Indeed," he replied. Jireh was about to cast the lifeless body into the water, when Velandris stopped him.

"Please, wait a second. Before you cast her away, lay her down so that I may show my respect to her... because she comes from the All Power, she is valued," said Velandris.

Jireh nodded his head and did as she asked. Velandris then removed all of her belongings and placed them on the body. "But why Velandris? She is truly hollow, there is nothing in there. She's just a spirit body. What is the purpose of this?" he asked.

"As you said, she is from the All Power but has nothing in this world. I want to honor her, just as you have honored me."

"I suppose. Very well then," said Jireh.

Velandris braided the hair of the empty body and grinned once she was done.

Jireh smiled at Velandris. "It seems you enjoyed giving to her more than keeping the gifts."

She then looked up at Jireh, "Perhaps it is better to give than to receive."

"Yes... I see that now," he replied.

"All done! However, she is still missing something," said Velandris.

"Other than a soul, I don't know what she's missing," he said.

"A name, what shall we call her?" asked Velandris.

"That's a good question. I'm not quite sure. If not a name, then perhaps a title of some sort?" Jireh suggested. "You have truly honored the All Power, Velandris. I am proud of you." He then summoned a small crystal and broke it in two. He took one part of the crystal and fused it within his chest and the other he placed in the right hand of the lifeless body. He then placed her left hand over her right hand.

With excitement Velandris landed on her feet and said, "I got it!" She kneeled and smiled at the body. "Someday, I hope we'll be able to meet you, somehow. I'm sure of it! Her name will have to wait but a title should fit her for now. So for what she is and all that she is, is a spirit."

Jireh kneeled and picked up the body and walked to the edge of the cloud.

"She is, The Holy Spirit," said Velandris.

Jireh kissed The Holy Spirit on her forehead and laid her in the living water. As the Holy Spirit sank down, Jireh softly said, "Farewell, Holy Spirit... for now." He removed his robe and placed it on Velandris, grabbed her hand and flew off in the distance.

CHAPTER 10
Born of Love

Six years had gone by since the Holy Spirit fell causing the Lords to grow weaker daily. They relied heavily on the Mana to restore them in the waking hours then rested at night because their bodies grew weary. Mornings were for farming the lands and gorging on Mana at the temple beneath the All Power. After eating they would adjust and modify the paradigm generator. The paradigm generator was a large crystal incubator designed to diffuse and materialize the spirit body, while expanding the soul and harnessing the All Power's power for a short period of time. Whoever is placed in the paradigm crystal will begin to materialize as soon as they enter the first layer of All Power.

The All Power has three layers not including the core. Once the paradigm crystal reaches the All Power's core, the energy transmitted will ignite the crystal, causing the soul and the core to fuse as one. The risk to this fusion becomes heightened because the crystal must have the dubitability to reach the All Power's core before the spirit body is completely materialized. Once the soul is exposed, the crystal will attach the soul to the All Power as one entity. The launch pad for the paradigm generator must have enough power to push the crystal to the core. The further the crystal goes, the tougher it is to push due to the intensity of the core. The Lord's ran test after test, but the device was nowhere near complete. None of the crystal models were robust enough to make it past the third layer. They thought that a diamond model would be better, but they feared that the diamond would be too strong and would materialize the spirit and soul too fast, taking a lot longer to ignite once entering the core. This would've been no problem for them in the past because they had the power to make any substance from matter; but they being stripped away from their power also stripped away the unlimited strength of their minds. They could have created the right material for the construction of this project, but they are now restricted and can only use the resources in which they have already created.

The Lords could not maintain their sync longer than five minutes nor could they share information or speak in unison and the All Power refused to bestow power onto them because of this. Syncing had become meaningless because it required too much energy to perform. It only exhausted them and required them to eat and drink after syncing. The twins Zuccaro and Nefartari were no longer allowed to stand beside one another because if the two were to automatically sync, they would lose their mind and become extremely violent.

After years of trying to perfect the paradigm generator, they grew tired of their failed results. Though they achieved high success rates they would not use the paradigm unless it were a one hundred percent success. They became increasingly frustrated and began to doubt their abilities. One Sunday, Jireh noticed that everyone's morale was down and decided that a break was needed.

"Brothers, we have worked the hardest we ever have, and we can feel the weariness in our bones. I believe now is the proper time to rest. We should rejoin when all are fully restored, both mentally and physically."

"No brother, we mustn't stop now, not when we're close to 100%," said Genesi.

Clave quickly interjected, "Brother Genesi, look at us, look at you. We're at our limits!"

It became quiet as all nodded their heads in agreement.

"Yes, go home brothers," Nicolette said. Make love to your wives and eat until your belly's are full."

"Is that all you think about? However, Arielle and I are planning to reproduce and make a child. I do not want to get involved with this project until my child is born," said Genesi.

Nicolette smiled and flew over to Genesi to pat him on the back. "Now you have the right idea... you dog you!" Nicolette laughed.

Annoyed, Genesi pushed Nicolette away with one arm, sending him flying into a lake outside of the temple. Genesi crossed his arms and turned away muttering "fool."

"Very well then. Do we all agree on taking a rest?" Cenci asked.

With his finger in the air, soaring out of the waters like a shooting star, Nicolette shouted, "I for one agree!"

"Agreed," said Kian Kiani.

"Yes, let us begin after the child of Genesi is born," said Genus.

All eventually agreed and just before they began the journey home, Nicolette posed a question. "Oh, just one more thing. Tell me, and please don't hold back thanking me, but how do you like my design of the mating ritual? Is it not better than you expected?"

Excitedly, they all began to speak at once, annoying Nicolette. "Clam down! One at a time, please!" he cried.

Genus stepping forward, cleared his throat, pushed his glasses up rightly onto his face and said, "Sorry my brothers, but it is best that I go first in the matter. How shall I say this, brother Nicolette, sex is... its... It may be the best thing since mana!!!"

Losing his calm composure and covering his face, Genus started giggling. Nicolette in turn covered his mouth as his chuckle attempted to escape. Cade then burst out in laughter pointing at Genus, "Look at him, it's so funny to see Genus lose himself!"

Genus pushed his glasses up and blushed, "Well, I can't help it. Sex is simply amazing; it is beyond the imagination and wow, what a sensation!"

"Yes, indeed it opens up all senses and places them at their highest levels, it's simply remarkable," said Cenci.

"OH YEAH! I love grabbing the breast and butt during sex, they're as soft as fresh clouds after a rainstorm," Cade noted droolingly.

Genesi crossed his arms and turned his back, "It's pleasurable, but you do not have my thanks."

"Rude!" said Nicolette. "Then you deserve to go without."

"That will never happen." Genesi argued.

"That's what I thought," said Nicolette.

Kian Kiani looked over at Jireh and noticed a meekness in his stance. "What about you, provider? How do you view the mating ritual?" said Kian Kiani.

The brothers collectively looked at Jireh with questions in their eyes. Jireh placed his hands behind his back and said, "I view the mating ritual as a sacred ceremony between the male and female Lord. It is the physical sync of expression towards your wife. It forms the physical bond between the two and releases all stresses."

Nicolette frowned, "Yuck! My goodness Provider, what kind of response is that?"

"Right! Boring! Come now Jireh, don't be so bashful! Give us the details!" said Cade.

Clave and Cenci both smiled at Jireh because they knew. Jireh immediately blushed and looked down.

Genesi stepped forward, "Well isn't it obvious? You haven't made love to your wife, have you?"

Genesi's outburst surprised Jireh. Jireh stepped forward to begin explaining, "Well, it's not that I don't want to, but I find her fascinating just as she is right now. She soothes my heart, and her gentleness brings rest to my ever-wandering mind. I fall in love with her every single day. She teaches me new things all the time... things I didn't even realize about myself. Perhaps I am enjoying our friendship so much that I don't feel it necessary to push the mating ritual. For us, I want it to be special and the right time. When we do meet, it will be the embodiment of our love and friendship... not just the first time, but every time we mate. Velandris is my second wind, she is my limbs. I'm truly enjoying every moment with her, and I believe that she feels the same way."

Cade and Nicolette were moved to tears as they wiped their eyes, they stood in awe of their brothers' words.

"Quite beautiful Jireh, may we all learn this type of compassion from you," said Cenci.

"I respect you, Jireh. You are unique in every way," Zuccaro agreed.

"I too have been selfish. I slept with my wife as soon as we had time alone... I really didn't know her," Nefartari said with shame shaking in his voice.

Kian Kiani immediately comforted him, "Don't feel down about it Nefartari, I believe we all did the same thing."

Genesi summoned the spirit energy around his body and took flight towards his temple. "Do as you please, Jireh. Mate with her or not, it matters nothing to me. The only thing that matters is my offspring. After that we can finish this wretched device. Now if you will excuse me, I am going home to mate with my wife!"

"Goodbye brother! Good Luck," yelled Nicolette and Cade.

Zuccaro, Cade, Nefartari, and Kian Kiani said their goodbyes and took flight.

Clave and Cenci waited for everyone to take off then immediately zoomed over to Jireh and bowed their heads.

Surprised by their actions, Jireh immediately questioned the gesture, "Why are you bowing your heads to me? We only bow to the All Power."

"No brother, we honor you!" said Cenci.

"We believe you are the perfect example for us all," Clave chimed.

Jireh, still confused, said, "I am doing as I've always done. My way has not changed since I've sprung from the All Power."

"And that way has always been good," said Clave.

"You are the closest of who we all once were, Jireh. You never changed! We can't help but to follow you. It is only right. You've always cared and knew what was right. You kept all of us in order," said Cenci.

"It is when we are together that brings order," Jireh corrected. "Brothers be who you are and stand true in your titles. I am the Lord of Light. Clave, Lord of Protection. Cenci, Lord of Understanding. Cade, is the Lord of Mischief. Nicolette, the Lord of Beauty. Kian Kiani, is the Lord of Ingenuity. Genus, the Lord of Intelligence. Nefartari and Zuccaro are the Lords of Zodiac, and Genesi is the Lord of Science."

"Yes, and we believe you are the best of us, and would like to learn under the Lord of the Light," said Clave.

While grateful for their words, Jireh was still taken back and so he rebuffed the pressure placed on him by his brothers. Jireh simply did not agree with them. "Brothers, I am glad that you believe in me, but you must not pick favorites. We are all one body and gifted with different talents. One is not greater than the other for we are all the same under the All Power."

Cenci decided it was his turn to make Jireh see reason. "Surely you are the best of us, brother. Was it not you that said that all who dwelled further away from the All Power have disobeyed thus, the reason our personalities changed? However, you never traveled far from the All Power. You even built your temple in perfect view of its auras!"

"I did in fact say that, however, it was only in theory. But the idea was not mine. It was once told to me by Zuccaro and Nefartari. In theory, the closer we are to the All Power, the more we stay in our original forms," said Jireh.

"Still Provider, we choose to imitate you!" Clave said.

Jireh sighed and saw that they could not see reason as they only heard what was in their hearts. "As you wish my brothers. I'm well pleased with all of you."

Clave and Cenci rejoiced at Jireh's response and bowed their heads.

"Well, I'm off for now. I love you and my peace I leave with you." said Jireh as he quickly took flight waving farewell.

A few thousand miles away, Velandris stood on top of a piece of floating land in the middle of the sea, gazing at one of the moons. It was pitch black out, but there accompanied by a slight breeze that flowed through her hair. The well-lit moon illuminated the sky with a light so stunning that one could see the colors of the wind with its ripples of purple, pink and yellow. Velandris randomly smiled and turned around to see Jireh a few yards away from her. He smiled back at her. "I knew that you'd be here, at the place where the ocean meets the sky. Tell me, what does this place do for you?" he asked.

"It is one of my favorite places in all of Heaven, but it does not make me happy. It only helps the time to pass by," said Velandris. She continued, "It's whenever I am with you! That's when I am happy, Lord Jireh."

As Jireh stood up and turned towards her, she immediately saw that something was amiss. With a sense of urgency Velandris shouted, "Karama!" In Karama's smallest form, he fell from Velandris' hair and landed on her shoulder. Karama yawned, then dashed towards Jireh. His body enlarged and wrapped around Jireh like a snake as Jireh collapsed on top of Karama.

Velandris sighed, "He's over worked."

Drowning Jireh with his wet tongue, Karama licked him repeatedly to keep him awake. Velandris then glided over to Jireh and gently grabbed his face. "My love-you look so weak. I've never seen you with such tired eyes," she said examining him.

"I was weak, but I only needed to find you, you who replenishes my strength" he said.

"You never had to look," Velandris countered as she picked up her husband and set him on Karama's back. "Karama, please take us home," she requested.

Karama opened his wings and bayed at the moon as he ran and jumped off the cliff beginning to soar. Velandris held Jireh in her arms as he kept his eyes fixed on her. "You are truly amazing and my most valued friend," He looked at her adoringly as she continued to clutch his body to hers.

Velandris's heart was filled. Unable to contain her excitement, her cheeks turned a bright blush as Jireh continued to sing her praises. "You are too good to me, my love. What mistakes can be found in you? Wife of mine. You are greater than I... SImply because they way that you are. It is the way you care for me; it is like the glorious rays of the All Power. That is what you and the All Power have in common. It's the power that you hold. The power of love! There are no ends to your love!"

Velandris, distracted, said, "Karama! Please boy, I know that you're excited, but I need to hear Jireh!" She looked to Jireh once more, "I'm sorry, what were you saying my love?"

Jireh chuckled, "I've only made one mistake in creating you."

"A mistake? Is there something wrong with me?" questioned Velandris.

"No, not at all. You're too perfect, you'll never understand. That's why we haven't made...," Jireh paused shyly. "If I could have given you one more gift, then it would be to give you the ability to see yourself through my eyes. Only then would you understand how special you are." Yawning, Jireh slowly closed his eyes and fell asleep.

Velandris beamed, leaned down and kissed him on the forehead, "You are mine forever, I will take care of you always, forever I promise."

***

It had been over one hundred years since the Lords worked on the paradigm generator. They had become comfortable with their new lives as their wives became each Lord's highlight. Nicolette and his wife were the first to give birth to a child and had nine more over the course of the fifty years. Both Nefetari and Zuccaro's wives had a set of twins. Genus and his wife had a son and a daughter who both sported glasses like Genus. Cade's three children were undoubtedly humorous and encouraged their parents to find new ways to improve on how to make the Lord's laugh. Cenci and his wife had six youngsters. Kian Kiani and his wife had five children while Clave's wife had too many kids to count.

Things were blissful and joyous. However, time revealed some unwelcome discoveries surrounding the female Lords. Most of their issues were minor like Cade's wife's horrible memory or Cenci's wife who slept more than any other wife. Velandris was unable to dream and Genesi's wife was barren. These issues would have been fixed easily if the Lords were restored to their original power. Sadly, their powers were constrained. Genesi hated the fact that he would never have a child with Adrielle and grew envious of his brothers. The distance he created between himself, and the fellow Lords made him delve deep into his work and experiments. He constantly used Adrielle and himself as guinea pigs to test out his newest experiments. Genesi had become skinny, and his face had sunken in making him less attractive than before. His bitterness and anger took over him, and his soul began to rot. He changed his outward appearance and wore a gold mask to cover his face and a black robe with gloves to cover his body to hide his disfigurations.

As Jireh stepped aside Velandris in bed, she couldn't help but beam with happiness. His voice and face were always refreshing to her especially after realizing that he was content with her and their life. They were so in sync they finished each other's sentences. The love they shared made it so that the two could not bear being away from one another for more than an hour. They spoiled each other with kindness and often resembled teenagers when discovering new levels of one another. They made eachother laugh and traveled all of Heaven seeking knowledge and teaching every step of the way. That night they had finished talking and were about to go to bed, but

Jireh felt the need to speak from his heart once again. "All this time, you have loved me correctly, and made me a better Lord...thank you," he said.

"Have I?" Velandris snapped back. She quickly hopped out of bed. "We're finishing each other's sentences all too often now. I refuse to stop here with you." She looked at Jireh with determination swimming in her eyes.

What's the matter?" Jireh asked. He was noticeably confused by Velandris' words.

"You and I!" she said.

Jireh shrugged his shoulders as her words were unexpected and he could not find the words to say at that moment.

Velandris sighed, "I knew you'd do that. Since you know me so well... come! Find me!"

Velandris immediately took flight, heading towards the sky. Jireh was confused. "What's gotten into her? Fine. Here I come," he said, taking flight. Velandris reached out her hand towards Jireh, stopping him from proceeding any further. "I did not say follow me. I said to find me," she said.

She balled up her fist and summoned a tornado of clouds that came and swept Jireh into the opposite direction. What has gotten into her? he thought. While engulfed in the tornado, He reached his hands out to his sides and yelled, "Enough!" The tornado submitted to Jireh's word and subsided. Jireh flew up and searched for Velandris. He called for her, but she did not answer, all he saw were the grassy plains and the light of the moons. Crossing his legs, he began to think. "Come find me," he said. He snapped his fingers, "I know!" He headed to the place where the ocean meets the sky. Upon his arrival, Jireh looked to the cliff where Velandris usually stood, but she was nowhere to be found.

"I don't understand. I just knew that she'd be here. There shouldn't be any other place she would go but here," he said aloud to himself. He turned his back and started to walk away from the cliff. Suddenly a long cloud landed on the cliff and there reappearing within the cloud was Velandris. Velandris spoke softly, looking up at the moon, "Jireh." Jireh turned around and saw Velandris' silhouette disappearing in the clouds. She then swung her hand out to her side, but her dress dematerialized into shimmers.

"Jireh come here please," she begged.

Jireh, shocked by what he was witnessing, said, "Of course."

As Jireh approached her, Velandris turned around to face him. "Jireh, I love you... but I have not loved you fully as your wife... you do not know all of me. Please come find me, so that I may know all of you."

Confused by her words, Jireh responded, "My lady, I have found you. I knew you'd be here."

Velandris took a step forward, grabbing his hand and placing it on her right breast. The clouds had completely dissolved at their shared touch revealing her naked body. Their eyes locked, neither one blinking. Velandris held out her other arm to the side and said, "Karama, go home boy." Karama fell from her hair and onto her shoulder. He yawned and then ran from her shoulder to her hand and took flight.

Jireh smiled and in a low sultry tone said, "I see!"

Jireh did not hesitate. He slowly placed his hand behind her ear and leaned forward. He then moved his hand to the back of her head, closed his eyes and kissed her with gentleness. Within that very moment they were once again in sync with one another. Their breath had become one as their minds searched the other for thoughts. As they kissed, Velandris slowly removed Jireh's robe and pants; and their bodies began to glow. A wind of mysterious lights appeared from the ground, circling them. Their power began to lift from the ground as their bodies had become feather-like. A smoother, stronger wind appeared that carried the two lovers over the sea.

That night they finally made love and truly discovered one another in all ways. From the beginning they were patient and kind. Their time spent made them more than husband and wife, they looked to each other as best-friends. They continued to flow within the innocence of their love taking their time in exploring their own universe. The wind carried them for seven days straight, and for seven straight days they did not stop making love.

***

It was the seventh week later did Velandris learned she was pregnant. Unlike modifying her pregnancy like the rest of the Lords, Jireh and Velandris decided to wait the entire seven year timeline enjoying the pregnancy process. An elixir was developed by Genesi and Adrielle to enhance the entire pregnancy process in six days but Jireh and Velandris decided against it. The enhanced pregnancy process allowed the Lords to collectively give birth to over a hundred children. Some married their cousins who gave birth as well.

Jireh and Velandris were a unit and made their decisions together. They would often tell the others, "The baby will come once it is ready. The pregnancy process must finish its perfect work so that it will be fully complete and lack nothing." When the birth of a new child occured, Jireh would go and bring all the Lords and their families together to celebrate. He often worried about Genesi's and Adrielle's feelings about children. Jireh and Velandris would often go to encourage them to keep trying but Genesi would dismiss Jireh's encouragement with facts and science.

The day had finally come for Velandris to give birth. Karama had flown to all the Heavenly kingdoms to give each Lord a handwritten scroll from Jireh. The Lords and their children's children gathered at Jireh's temple, with gifts and food. The Female Lords rushed to Velandris' aid with support and encouragement.

"Please, go tell Jireh that I can no longer wait. The child is ready now," said Velandris. Cleo Clave went and did as her sister asked, summoning Jireh. Shortly after, the Lords entered Jireh's bedroom. They lined up parallel to one another as Jireh walked in between them. With tears in his eyes, Jireh grabbed Velandris' hand and reassured her, "I am here."

Velandris forced a smile, looked in between her legs and took a deep breath squeezing Jireh's hand. Velandris pushed with little to no effort and out came their child with its thumb in its mouth. The tears in the room were not that of the newborn baby but from Jireh and Velandris. The Lord's thought it strange that the child did not come out crying but was at peace. Clave picked up the child shouting, "It is a boy, a baby boy!" Jireh and Velandris wept with joy as everyone surrounding them rejoiced. There was a glow that came from the child that offset the Lord. They all instantaneously recognized the energy from the glow surrounding the child, but could not find the words to explain what they felt.

"What is this light that comes from that child?" asked Genesi.

The room became silent as they looked to one another for answers.

Clave quickly handed the child to Velandris and yelled "Congratulations, my sister and brother."

The baby was so small that he fit perfectly in Velandris' hand. Filled with love and joy, said, "At long last. He is here, Jireh. This is my gift to you...a son," Velandris said heartfeltly.

"Our son," he said while wiping his tears.

"He is very handsome," Clave noted.

Jireh gushed over his new son. "Yes, he has acquired his mother's beauty. Green eyes and green hair too."

"But he has the color of your skin," Velandris said... "The skin of the All Power."

"Indeed, it is. It's a boy though, I was hoping for a girl. We surely cannot use the name Joanna that I was planning," Jireh joked. "Perhaps the name Adam since it's a boy?" Jireh suggested.

"Adam Jireh. It's nice but in honor of your name, let's use the letter 'J'," Velandris said.

"Hmmm, with all the time that has passed, I have not prepared a name for a boy. The choice is yours, Velandris."

Velandris smiled at her baby and said, "You have already blessed us. You who are greater than I am. The one who is the joy of us, the child born of love, son of Jireh. You shall be called Jehovah Jireh. Like the one before you, you shall provide."

CHAPTER 11
Abel's Determination

"You shall be called Jehovah Jireh. Like the one before you, you shall provide," said Adam.

Abel was amazed by what he heard. With excitement he turned to Cain but did not see him. "Cain? Cain? Where did he go?" asked Abel.

A strong wind came and knocked Abel down immediately. At that moment, Abel felt something wrong in his spirit. "Something isn't right. I can feel it. When did he leave? He was right beside me Abel thought to himself," he thought.

He stood up and looked around. "Brother... Brother!" he yelled.

Abel grabbed Adam's robe and shook him. "Dad, Dad! Snap out of it! Something is wrong!" Abel yelled.

But Adam did not respond, as he continued with the story.

"Come on Dad! I need your help please, wake up!" Abel begged.

"As much as he talked about this day. He would never leave in the middle of a story. Maybe he is with mother," said Abel. Abel quickly left his dad and ran to Eve to find her sleeping just as before. Then a stronger wind came and pushed him towards the forest.

"The forest? Ok, I'll go there," Abel thought.

Abel kissed his mother and dashed away. As he entered the forest, he began to call for his brother, but once again there was no response. Only the echoes of wildlife were heard to which they responded to Abel's call saying, "Danger, danger leave now."

Abel searched for over two hours and by this time had become lost in the forest. Out of breath, he leaned up against a tree for a moment of rest. However, worry swarmed his heart, so he began shouting even louder for his brother, but there was no response. Hunger and thirst began to set in as he realized the forest had become eerily quiet.

Suddenly, an apple fell from the tree that he stood under. Without hesitation, Abel picked up the apple and was surprised by what he witnessed. The apple had the name "Adam" carved into it with a bitten chuck missing. Immediately after, he heard the laughter of a female voice swarming all around him. Abel looked around but could see nothing.

"An apple stays within the shadows of the tree from which it falls," the woman's voice told him.

Abel dashed away from the tree and looked up to see who was speaking. The figure swiftly leapt from tree to tree, circling Abel as all he could see was her constantly darting silhouette though he could sense her energy, for it was of blood lust.

"No normal cavewoman can move like this, only that of a Maylen man! You are not of God! Show yourself, demon!" yelled Abel.

She laughed, "Don't rush your death human!"

"In the name of Jehovah Jireh, I command you to show yourself, now!" he shouted.

Abel heard a loud scream from the demon. Then the screams became that of a distorted lion's roar. As she yelled, the entire forest went up in flames. Abel immediately went into his fighting stance as he summoned blue spirit around his body.

"Demon! Are you to blame? Where is my brother!" hollered Abel.

A fireball then shot out from the flames behind him, quickly taking notice; Abel threw a punch and extinguished the fireball with his fist. Three more fireballs shot down from the sky, four more from his left, and three more from his right. Abel soared and thrusted both of his hands forward to create a strong barrier of air around him to extinguish the flames. As his feet touched the ground, the parade of fireballs continued but he quickly dodged them using punches to extinguish each host of fire.

Abel could hear her unnerving laugh throughout the forest.

The demon began to taunt Abel again.

"How long can you keep this up... Maylen boy?" she said.

"Until I end it! And this ends now!" Abel yelled. Abel placed his hands together jumping into the air. Green flames engulfed his hands as he spun his body around in a full 360-degree motion. He instantly opened both hands and stretched them at his sides yelling, "Holy Power, Noble Wind!" With intense energy and focus, Abel unleashed a destructive wave of wind from his body, destroying all things within a three-hundred-yard radius. The wind extinguished the rest of the flames left in the forest. Abel landed on the ground and immediately went back into his fighting stance.

"Now, may there be no more hiding... come out and tell me where Cain is!" he demanded.

Again, Abel heard her uncanny laugh coming from the northern part of the forest. He turned and saw a figure walking out of the forest with glowing yellow eyes the color of a freshly lit campfire. The figure opened her wings and removed the dust and smoke surrounding her. Walking slowly and seductively toward him, her long jet-black hair swung from side to side. Steeply floating behind her back was her flaming Trident. Placed on her hip was a whip and a long with a flamed tip. Her beautifully toned purple body was complemented by dragon scales in all but a few areas on her body from her gargantuan wings down to her hooved feet used to trudge around the forest.

"Who are you?" Abel asked again.

"You'd know if you stayed with Adam. Respectfully, it is only right that you know the name of the one who is about to kill you," she responded.

"Then you should know that my name is Abel," he said.

She smiled and said, "Cute and clever... I am the Queen Succubus, Lilith!"

"I've never heard of you," Abel retorted.

"Of course, you haven't. Adam has kept many secrets from you," said Lilith.

Abel quickly ran to the defense of his dad saying, "My Dad is a wise man and holds what he needs to be held."

"Because of Adam you are a fool from birth. I am going to kill and enslave everyone who has betrayed me and unfortunately for you, you're on my list!" said Lilith.

"I don't know what you're talking about! But I believe that none of this is a coincidence! You have the answer that I'm looking for. Where is my brother Cain?" Abel demanded.

"With the Satan, obviously," she replied starkly.

"What?" He asked. Abel could not contain his shock at Lilith's words.

"You humans are all the same. You're blind! He is a jealous one! Let the Satan have him and I will kill him and the Satan for you," said Lilith.

"I don't believe a word from you. Cain is my brother. Watch what you say about him!" yelled Abel.

Lilith snapped her head to meet Abel's gaze, "I do not lie! You and I both know that Cain wants more power. As to why, I do not know, nor do I care."

"You're lying, Cain wouldn't side with the Satan," Abel protested.

"Whether you believe me or not, I do not care. Your fate is still the same," said Lilith.

"But you do know where he is?" Abel asked.

"Of course. I see everything on this planet. Every cursed thing," she replied.

"Then if that's the case, here is my proposition. If I defeat you, you'll tell me where Cain is?" said Abel.

Lilith smiled devilishly and said, "You're bold... I like it." Lilith licked her lips and said, "If you think you can, sure I'll tell you, but I have come a long way! Once you are defeated, I will kill the rest of your family and then the one who betrayed me..."

"I won't allow it! I won't hold back!" Abel began to summon his spirit power and Lilith noticed a sharp turn in Abel's demeanor as the ground began to shake. Abel cried out as his body began to be filled with light.

"I won't give you the chance," yelled Lilith as she teleported in front of Abel. Speedily, Lilith grabbed Abel by the throat and lifted him off the ground. As his feet dangled in mid-air, she cocked back using her free fist and punched Abel in the stomach. Her blow caused blood to fly from Abels mouth and land on her breasts. With her grip released, she threw a barrage of punches to Abel's face, chest, arms, and legs, viciously beating on him. "You thought I'd sit back and allow you to get stronger? You buffoon! Your first mistake was not being prepared," she laughed. Lilith then took her tail and choked him as she beat on Abel's body.

"What a shame! I thought a human would be stronger!" she yelled at him tauntingly.

Abel struggled to free himself from the firm grip of her tail.

Bored with simply beating on Abel, Lilith grew angrier and began screeching from frustration. "Is this it! I am not pleased. Is your God not seeing this? Where is your guardian angel? I've come so far... where are they? I need someone stronger to fight! yelled Lilith.

Abel could not reply, nor could he see anything due to the wounds above his eye.

"Must I kill everyone so that you may hear my cry!" Lilith continued.

Frustrated, Lilith slammed Abel into the ground and loosed her grip from Abel's neck. She then dashed up taking flight toward the sky.

As she turned around and met Abel's partially shut eyes, Lilith began, "They will remember me. They will see me again and they will regret what they have done to me. I will get their attention with your blood! I am going to bury you there permanently." Lilith screamed as she struck down like lightning, impaling Abel deep into the ground using his own fist.

Then the Satan's curse came on her causing her demeanor to change. As Lilith pressed into Abel all the force she could muster, she couldn't keep her eyes off him. She admired the beauty of his face and stared at him seductively which peaked her constant craving for sex. Lilith temptingly licked her lips. "You handsome little boy you. Do you feel the tension? Do you feel the pressure from my breasts against you?" asked Lilith. She then shook her head and yelled at herself to focus. She instead began another round of relevant questions. "Does it hurt?" she asked, punching Abel in the face. Abel was dazed from Lilith's onslaught, but in his mind, he was calm as he patiently waited.

Lilith grinned, "Good! I prefer your silence over your words! I am finally beginning to enjoy myself! You see, usually I sleep with my enemies to kill them. But this right here is rare! It's seldom that I get to fight! My perfect body wilds them, brings them in and when I climax, my fluids shatter their spirit! But you, I want to rip you apart!"

Abel began to struggle as he tried to guard himself against her punches but the extreme pressure from Lilith's assault delayed his actions. Now deep within the ground, Lilith randomly paused her attack.

Arousing herself, Lilith licked her lips and said, "I want to enjoy every moment, little boy." She leaned forward to smell the blood running down the side of Abel's mouth. "What a delightfully rich smell." She looked into Abel's eyes and smirked. "I will enjoy this smell more when l bask in your blood. But first..." she said. Lilith reached for Abel's belt buckle and began to pull down his pants. He firmly grabbed Lilith's wrist and in a deep low tone said, "That's only for my wife."

Lilith laughed and said, "Wife? Little boy you are deep underground, but don't you worry! You will not die a virgin today."

Abel then spit the remaining blood from his mouth and said, "If I die today, it will not be by you. Little do you know; you have given me the vantage point."

"You are sadly mistaken," she said.

"No, I am sure of myself. Look around you! We are deep in the ground, where dirt reigns. Am I not my father's son? Adam, my earthly Dad was made from the dirt! I too am of that dirt!" Abel materialized into dirt and became one with the soil.

Lilith was astounded by Abel's sudden escape as she smashed her fist in the dirt. Quickly realizing that she was at a disadvantage, she darted toward the entrance, but seconds later the soil engulfed and smothered Lilith. The extreme pressure from the surrounding ground began to crush her. Dirt poured into her mouth, clogged her ears, and choked her. She filled with so much muck that she began to bloat. Lilith panicked and fought against the overwhelming power of the earth. She summoned all her power and sent forceful waves of energy from her body, forcing the dirt off her. A massive crater was left within the forest as Lilith flew up and out of the ground. She took flight, afraid to touch the ground again keeping her distance. She became sick and threw-up the dirt into one pile. As she clamored for air, Abel formed himself from the same dirt Lilith regurgitated.

Fully healed from the wounds gifted to him by Lilith, Abel looked up at her and took his fighting stance. "Foolish demon, look around you. Do you not know where you are? Was it not God that gave us dominion here?" said Abel.

"Shut up!" Lilith yelled.

"I've give you some credit for trying, but the battle was over from the beginning. Demon, you underestimate God and my abilities... you see I was prepared, God sent angels to train me"

Enraged, Lilith howled and shrieked at the truth Abel pointed out.

"This ends now," he said. Abel opened his arms and transformed into his spirit body. Immersed in blue power and energy, his skin and eyes glowed like a cerulean gemstone. Seven golden fiery swords appeared next to him. The swords slowly circled Abel as he went back into his fighting stance.

Terrified, Lilith gasped. "The Seven house weapons of Jireh! How is that possible for a man?" Lilith thought.

Lilith felt Abel's power increase and became increasingly overwhelmed. Abel's intentions to kill her caused her to quickly power down and lower her guard.

Surrendering, Lilith spoke, "That is enough for now! You have won!" She shattered into hundreds of miniature bats and disbursed into all directions.

Before the last black creature disappeared, Abel heard, "Your brother is going to sell his soul to Lucifer. Go now! Head north towards Mount Hermon. If you survive, know that I am coming for you, son of man. This is far from over! You will surely see me again."

Abel could no longer feel her presence and dismissed his swords. However, Lilith's words troubled Abel. Fear swept over him as stress overtook his body.

"I will stop him!" Abel said aloud. I need to tell Dad, but I don't have enough time, he thought. Abel looked around and saw a falcon off in the distance. Acting fast, he cried out, "You there! Bird, come here." The bird did as Abel commanded and flew to him.

"Little one, I need you to deliver something to my mother, Eve. You will find her near the Jordan river. Abel transformed his left pinky finger into soil and removed it. He spoke into the dirt and placed it into the mouth of the falcon. He then blessed the falcon and sent it on its way. Moments later a swift and aggressive wind came and guided Abel north.

"He can't be more than an hour or so ahead of me. At full speed, I can reach him!" said Abel as he took off running.

***

Near the Maylen camp site, Eve woke up to see Adam under a tree in his tranced state. She was concerned because Adam was telling the Origins' story but their sons were nowhere to be found. She went over to Adam and softly touched his sweat filled face. She then looked around and became extremely disturbed. "Something is wrong, the boys waited years to hear the Alpha story..." she said.

She then turned and looked at Adam only to hear, "Jehovah Jireh, now seven hundred years old, stood at the altar patiently waiting for his bride."

CPSIA information can be obtained
at www.ICGtesting.com
Printed in the USA
LVHW031211241121
704330LV00007B/176